Babe Ruth
Is Missing

Babe Ruth
Is Missing

An Ovid Kent Novel

Saul Isler

POCAMUG PRESS™

Pocamug Press™
May's Lick, Kentucky

Version 6/24/17

Library of Congress Control Number: 2017944191

ISBN: 9780998479019

For

Bill Isler

At exactly 3:20 a.m., in a San Francisco mansion, a second-floor bedroom window shatters. A tall man stands in the darkened room. He waits for a reaction from its sole occupant. Soft, continuous breathing suggests that the occupant's sleep has not been disturbed. The tall man wears white latex gloves. He plays a penlight on the walls, its narrow beam settling upon a framed montage containing two photos, a pair of ticket stubs and a small sheet of autographs. After silently removing the screws that anchor the montage to the wall, the tall man removes the montage, slips it into a pillowcase and, with the pillowcase, makes a quick exit. At a few minutes after ten the next morning, the occupant awakens and looks for the montage, as is his habit. He immediately sees that it is missing. He frantically searches for it in his closet, under his bed, in the most incongruous of places. He does not find it but he does, at last, notice the broken window. He sits on his bed and begins to moan. The moan grows to an inhuman, heartrending wail, a sound not unlike that of a male gorilla who has just lost his mate.

Part I.

San Francisco

1.

It was the sunset that did it, the outrageous way it ignited the Golden Gate Bridge before settling itself into the placid Pacific as delicately as a dowager aunt entering the shallow end of a pool. That sunset, framed by that golden-red span across the safe harbor of San Francisco, is, beyond any other, the reason I put my case dollar into this houseboat. In Sausalito, just north of the Bridge, you pay for a view like this by the square foot and through the nose.

But I got lucky. The DEA accepted my knocked down bid for this home on the bay as a reward for past service; specifically, as a favor for my saving the jobs, if not the lives, of two of my fellow agents during a RICO bust of the Mexican drug lord who used the boat as his big city toy. He's now doing life at San Quentin, just up the bay. Hell, all I did was sneak under a rataplan of AK-47 firepower and slice the front tires of the baddys' getaway car before they jumped in it to escape. A story I'll save for another time. These days are nothing like the old DEA days. Which is what I like about them.

This place is where I live and where I work. It's the first kind of permanence I've ever had. If I've never planted roots, at least I've cast an anchor.

2.

I'm sitting in my bolted-down, Naugahyde La-Z-Boy on the back deck of my *Bernie*. That's what I named my digs. Not as interesting or titillating a moniker as the *Best Revenge* or *Kubla Khan* or *Wet Dream* that identify the houseboats around me, but Bernie was my late dad, a very good guy. It's a good way to remember him.

I'm casting for Doris, the biggest damn sturgeon in the Bay. Everyone knows her, none have ever caught her. She's named after the sea god Poseidon's wife. Though I've never left water's edge, I've been after her for two years. Sturgeons kind of like the shore.

The sun is dousing itself beneath the GG when my phone starts ringing. It's nearly seven p.m. and I figure it for a telemarketer. I don't have Caller ID, not even call-waiting. I wouldn't own a phone if I didn't need one to make a buck. My twenty-inch TV is on the fritz and I'm all thumbs on my MacBook. But business hasn't been so great lately, and it might be a prospective client wanting me to chase down a spare copy of the Magna Carta or something. I grab the call.

"Kent here."

"Ovid Kent?"

"That's me."

"Ovid Kent Rare Books & Autographs?"

"The same." How many Ovid Kents does this guy think there are?

"This is Milton Blackstone." The tone suggests I should know the man's name. "I secured your number from a mutual acquaintance, your former DEA department head, Bert Jonsson. Recommended you highly because of your specialized background."

Specialized background? Good ol' Swede Jonsson, I say to myself. Blackstone has a quavery voice but excellent diction. An Englishman's English without being an Englishman. Old man. I *should* know his name. Pin it down in a minute. "I'm listening, Mr. Blackstone. Is there something I can help you with? Doesn't sound like you care to wait till normal business hours. An out-of-print book, an autograph, perhaps? "

"Autograph, Mr. Kent?" he snorts. "I guess you might say that. But not one I wish to buy. Or sell. I have a problem, an unusual and most troubling problem about which I would like to speak with you privately and in person." The voice pauses. "I require your services, sir. The matter is urgent. Most urgent."

What does Blackstone mean about an autograph he doesn't want to buy *or* sell? Is there a fee here? If so, that "most urgent" could add a few bucks to it. "Mr. Blackstone," I say, "is there anything you can tell me over the phone?"

"A great deal, sir, but, no, I'd prefer to do so face-to-face. I most often retire early, but I'd appreciate your meeting with me this very evening. Say, have you dined yet?"

No point in trying to impress this Milton Blackstone with how terribly busy I am. "No, Mr. Blackstone, I haven't. Do you live in the city?"

"I do, indeed."

"Then just give me the particulars, I can be there by eight or so."

Doris is safe for another day.

I jot Blackstone's directions on my yellow legal pad and thank him for calling. Then I prop my size twelves on my desk and sweep the dust bunnies from the corners of my mind. Blackstone, Blackstone? Nothing comes to me. I fire up my Mac.

Milton Blackstone, Esquire. Once, the most feared and respected trial lawyer in California, maybe the nation. Was the first to handle multi-million dollar palimony cases for movie stars, which he did as a sideline. Got LA's notorious Hilltop Killer a wrist-slap ten-to-twenty on a plea bargain. Defended a sea piracy case that earned him the pirated tanker as his fee. The last case he lost was a mock trial in his senior year at Yale. Thank you, Wikipedia.

I'm properly impressed. What surprises me is that this legend—his courtroom prowess earned him the moniker "Blackstone the Logician"—is still alive and functioning. The man has to be in his late eighties, maybe nineties.

He lives, I realize, in the Sea Cliff district fifteen minutes from me, overlooking both the ocean and the bay. Pure swank. I'm not sure what's in it for me, but I'm whistling *We're Off to See the Wizard* before I hit the shower.

3.

San Francisco is Manhattan with hills, but without the neat grid of streets. A great place to live, but you wouldn't want to park here. Sea Cliff, however, has no parking problems. Hasn't *any* problems. It's perched on the northern slope of San Fran, separated from the frenzy of the city by the fragrant eucalyptus woods of the Presidio. El Camino Drive runs from elegant four-story townhouses to bloated mansions with cherubed gates.

Number twelve is in the latter category.

"Ovid Kent," I say to the gate's squawk box as the sun has about set. Recognizing me, it rolls itself open. Regretting that I didn't have time to run my ancient black PT Turbocruiser through a wash, I hide it at the end of the U-shaped drive, then walk back and press the button next to the massive front door. What I hear from inside is Big Ben's brother. With just enough time to check my reflection in the door's cut glass panel, I run my hand through my mop of silver hair, adjust my argyle pocket square and hitch my slightly wrinkled cords over my own little problem which Dr. Atkins—you remember Dr. Atkins?—and I are working on as I speak. Never mind that sartorial correctness is not my strong suit. I've led myself to believe that I have a certain flair for draping my person.

"Welcome to Overlook, Mr. Kent," orates the stately man who opens the door. The house has a name? I'm impressed all over again, but the place *is* impressive. And it overlooks the entire Bridge and enough of the ocean to see the far-away Farallon Islands even in the dying light of this promising early-October day.

"I am Thomas," the man pronounces. I hand him the bottle of decent red I'd grabbed from my neighbor, Ethel, along with my slightly bent business card. He eyes the bottle with disdain, holding it out like it's a bag of poodle droppings. Lucky it wasn't Two-Buck-Chuck. He deigns not to look at the card, then peeks at it, rejecting, by a slight turn of his head and marked downturn of his lipless mouth, its obviously false provenance. This must be Milton Blackstone's butler or valet. I don't know the difference, but his British accent appears more authentic than his master's. Is Thomas his last name or first? The way he speaks tells me he can be deferential without being subservient.

"Mr. Blackstone is waiting to see you in the conservatory with young Mr. Blackstone."

Yeah, yeah, and Colonel Mustard's in the library with the knife.

"Please follow me."

Right. Should I "walk this way?" Get serious, Kent, you're here on serious business. So I follow Thomas to a bay-windowed atrium filled with exotic plants and trees, some of which nearly reach the twenty-foot glass ceiling. At the end of the room is a very old man who looks as delicate as the antique Biedermeier desk at which he's seated. He wears a velvet smoking jacket and a perfectly arranged silk ascot tucked into a tan cashmere sweater. The man's liver-spotted hands, with a rock of a diamond displayed on his pinky, are clasped and resting on the tooled leather of the desk. "Dapper" is the descriptor that comes to me.

4.

Opposite the desk is a love seat occupied by a pear-shaped man likely in his mid-sixties. He is sitting uncomfortably erect. The man's tonsured skull, his remaining hair still mostly black, is lowered. His eyes are focused on his hands, held palms up in his lap. He's dressed in a loud plaid jacket that looks out-of-place on him and he wears a white dress shirt buttoned at the neck, but no tie. I'm guessing the look of anguish on his face is permanent. His knees are held tightly together, his heavy brown brogans, slightly spread, point inward. He is almost imperceptibly rocking back and forth as if in prayer. A beautiful Doberman lies disinterestedly at his feet.

He is there, yet he is not there.

"Mister Kent, I'm Milton Blackstone," says the old man. "Welcome to our home. We call it Overlook. Doesn't overlook much, does it?" His grin reveals perfect white teeth. Obviously not his own.

I laugh dutifully at this joke he must have told a million times. The old man turns to the middle-aged man. "This, sir, is my son, John. John, please say hello to Mr. Ovid Kent. And this, sir, is our Stinson, the four-legged member of the family. Mr. Kent has come to help us find Babe Ruth."

Babe Ruth? I can't wait to hear what this is all about.

John Blackstone's response is, if clearly enunciated, practically inaudible. "Hello, Mr. Kent." The words are delivered to his hands. He does not look at me. He doesn't seem able to. Stinson pulls himself to his feet, strolls over to me, sniffs my crotch, then strolls back to lie again at John's feet.

"Hello, John, I'm pleased to meet you. I hope you'll both call me Ovid." The elder Blackstone looks at me questioningly. "It's the name my mother gave me," I say. "She loved to read Greek literature. Loved to read, period. She demanded that her only child read constantly, which is something I first resisted, but later was deeply grateful for." I wasn't here to talk about me, but I wanted to break the ice. Blackstone's stare tells me no ice is breaking, so maybe I'd better just shut up and listen.

"I trust you won't mind, Mr. Kent, but I'm hopelessly old-fashioned. I prefer 'Mister' Kent, but I'm certain my son will be happy to refer to you as Ovid if you wish."

Happy? John Blackstone's blank, unsmiling face suggests he couldn't be happy winning the lottery. Not that he'd ever need to.

"I must inform you, Mr. Kent, that John is often seen as what was once called an idiot savant. The term has become a pejorative one. His behavior is typical of one who suffers from that difficult condition, now known clinically as Asperger's Syndrome; if it could be said that he suffers at all."

Blackstone is talking about his son as though he isn't in the room. He goes on. "There's a general impression that Asperger's carries with it superior intelligence and a tendency to become deeply interested in, even preoccupied with, a particular subject."

"Isn't Asperger's like autism?" I ask.

"There are marked similarities, sir, even to Tourette's Syndrome. All are often misunderstood. In referring to John, I prefer to avoid labels. He is my son, sir, and I love him dearly."

Blackstone surprises me, speaking bluntly of John's condition in one breath, then sentimentally in another.

"Mr. Blackstone, isn't it also common for one with John's condition to exhibit exceptional skills in the narrow field of his interest?"

"Excellent observation, Mr. Kent. How did you know that?

"Like my mother, I read, too."

"I'm impressed, sir. I have a feeling we're going to get along very well. Regarding John, I must say that, at the moment, he most definitely is suffering, but not from his condition. He lives easily with that. It's for a very different reason. His most valuable possession is missing. Stolen, burgled, as it were: his autographs of Babe Ruth, along with two other Hall of Fame players, Ty Cobb and Tris Speaker. The names were on a single, small, loose-leaf page. These names are familiar to you, sir?"

Is he kidding? "Of course, Mr. Blackstone." I'm beginning to get where he's going. I'm also beginning to pick up on his odd habit of using the word *sir*. Very Victorian. Very Trollope.

"The page was mounted in a framed montage which included a large photo of Mr. Ruth, another of Mr. Ruth with John, and a pair of ticket stubs from the baseball game at which . . . well, John will eventually give you the details. It was this montage that was removed from John's bedroom wall as we all slept last night, then, I presume, was removed from the premises. Retrieve it, Mr. Kent, and I'll reward you handsomely."

"Mr. Blackstone," I say, "I'm not a detective and—as you know—I'm no longer with the DEA. I used to chase bad guys, I don't anymore."

"You'll simply be 'chasing'—as you put it—signatures, a small sheet of autographs. That *is* what you do, is it not?"

"Why, yes, sir, that is precisely what I do, but—"

"Twenty-five thousand dollars, Mr. Kent. That's what I'll pay for their return. Plus, of course, any expenses you may incur in your search."

My head nods my assent for a full ten seconds before I respond. I need to hang on to my cool here. "You're most convincing, Mr. Blackstone. I must say that money like that speaks. It tells me that I can and will find your John's missing Babe Ruth, sir."

He's already got me saying it.

But what the hell kind of crazy promise did I just make to Sir Blackstone?

5.

It takes me three, four months to make twenty-five grand dealing rare books and sigs. How can a set of baseball autographs, even a set that includes Babe Ruth's, be worth anywhere near what he's just offered?

"I have to tell you, Mr. Blackstone, these days, Babe Ruth's signature, on paper anyhow, goes for five thousand, tops. I can replace yours for, I'm guessing, four. So, though you may think me foolish for questioning your largesse, out of courtesy to you I must."

"Thank you, I understand, Mr. Kent, but the intrinsic or market value of the autographs does not concern me. Look, I'm being a terrible host. Dinner will be ready shortly and I haven't offered you a libation. I'm not allowed more than a small sherry, but perhaps you'd like something a little stronger?"

The question triggers my gin buds. But I'd had my martini earlier. At a time like this I don't need to bend my antennae. "Sherry will be fine, thank you, sir." Thomas is dispatched to "Bring the Tio Pepe."

"While we're sipping, Mr. Kent, allow me to explain why John considers these particular autographs so valuable. You see, he personally secured them from Mr. Ruth, Mr. Cobb and Mr. Speaker. He was a boy of eleven or twelve at the time—I believe it was June of 1947—and the occasion took place in Cleveland."

15

"Cleveland?" I blurt. That's where I'm from."

The mention of the city immediately brings a rush of memories. Of my father, an accountant—a bookkeeper actually —who'd been something of a cipher, a sweet and loving though ineffectual being. And of my mother who had so influenced my early years, but then suddenly disappeared. From my life, from my dad's. It was almost as if she'd died. She had, in fact, run off with another man, the bastard!

Blackstone looks blankly at me for a few seconds. "That's good to hear, Mr. Kent. Who knows but that your quest may take you back there. If it does, it may help that you know your way around. Anyhow, as I was saying before you so good-naturedly interrupted me, John was with me in Cleveland where I was taking a deposition in a murder trial. Because of his love for— and remarkable knowledge of—baseball, I often took him along on my travels during his summer vacations. Especially when I visited Major League cities. If possible, while there, we'd take in a ballgame or two. Baseball is of little interest to me, but it is— if I may say—all of life to John.

"Look, sir, it's important that you hear the whole story directly from him. He doesn't speak much, you know, but he's told that particular story hundreds of times to just about anyone who'll listen. It's good therapy for him. But I suggest we save it for after dinner. Thomas has prepared a lovely standing rib for us. With Yorkshire pudding, of course."

So Thomas cooks, too, I note. Does he burgle as well? Did the butler do it? Though no more than a clichéd possibility, I'd pursue it nevertheless. I'm more than ready to get to work, more than I am to eat, but I'm a sucker for good prime rib.

At that moment, as if on cue, Thomas appears from behind a ficus to announce that dinner is ready. Immediately, Milton Blackstone rolls himself from behind the desk and leads the long trek to the spacious dining room.

I've been put so at ease with Blackstone's engaging manner,

I hadn't noticed he's in a wheelchair. I can easily imagine him charming a jury the same way.

The meal ends with a nonpareil trifle, scooped out for us by the ever-present Thomas. Throughout, no mention has been made of the missing montage. Milton Blackstone, telling courtroom stories, is a talking history book. John Blackstone keeps to himself, hardly eating. His mind is elsewhere. The way his hands have suddenly become animated, he must be rehearsing the telling of his oft-told tale. Throughout his father's stories I step out of character to listen more than talk.

Afterward, Blackstone suggests we retire to the library where "John can take us back to the day he met Mr. Ruth." He actually seems anxious to hear what he must have heard too many times to count. His love for his son is apparent. I'm beginning to like this man. My kind of guy. But with a whole lot more than my kind of money.

Once in the library, he reaches into a desk drawer and withdraws a bottle of forty-five year old Amontillado sherry—a favorite of Poe's—and a pair of exquisite crystal snifters. He pours it as if it's a cheap table wine.

"This is my secret cache, Mr. Kent. If Thomas knew of it he'd never forgive me." Thomas, I'm certain, knows of it, keeps the bottle filled and likely forgives his employer daily for partaking of same. I know I'm in for a long evening. This is okay. I am truly enjoying it. And it's Blackstone's dime.

6.

The old lawyer then extracts two sheets of paper and places them on the desk. Handing me the first sheet, Blackstone says, "This is the montage, sir. That is, a photograph of it. And this is an enlarged copy of its most important feature, the sheet of autographs, the object you'll be seeking even if the rest of the montage cannot be recovered. I'd like you to retrieve the entire montage, but it's the sheet of signatures that truly matters."

The copy of the sigs clearly delineates the outlines of the original autographed page. The original was a lined sheet of three-hole loose-leaf paper measuring four by six inches. On it, sideways, are the three autographs. No good wish from Ty Cobb, just his parsimoniously scritched name in faded green ink, crammed into the upper left corner. Must have used his own pen. In faded blue, at the diametrically opposite corner is the neatly penned name of Tris Speaker. In the middle of the page, writ large and also in blue, is the most coveted autograph in sports history: "Sincerely, Babe Ruth." The beautiful Spenserian writing is unexpected, coming from a big, rollicking ape like the Babe. Other than John Hancock's familiar scrawl, it might be one of the best-known signatures in America. Every kid in the country, in his day and long, long after, had a bat, ball or glove with his name inscribed on it.

I presume, from the way the Babe's autograph grabs the

center of the page—not surprising for the ego he was known to have—that he'd signed first, leaving little room for the others. I can picture the signing scene, but I don't have to try, I'm about to have it described to me, likely in minute detail.

❏

John Blackstone now sits on a straight-backed chair across from the desk. I face him in an identical chair opposite. His hands are clasped around a glass of milk he's brought with him from the dining room. He looks into it as if to divine its contents.

"John," his father says, "if you're comfortable, won't you please tell Mr. Kent what happened in Cleveland when you met Mr. Ruth and his friends?"

John turns and stares vacantly at his father. He looks as if he doesn't understand the question. Finally, collecting himself, he speaks two words. "Yes, Father."

Then, the younger Blackstone, again rocking back and forth, tells the story of the most important day of his life, a day that occurred more than half a century earlier.

7.

"Lunch, Father. You told me to go to lunch. It was Saturday, June the twenty-first, 1947. It was nearly noon and you told me to go to lunch." He speaks precisely in a soft monotone, pausing for prompting by his father.

"Please continue, John. Tell Mr. Kent the story all the way to the end."

I'm anxious to probe for the details of the previous evening's theft, but I'm certain to need this background. Questions later, now I listen.

John doesn't speak to me, as requested, but to his father. The old man seems to expect this and does nothing to divert this oddly misdirected delivery. "You were busy talking to a client in our hotel room. You asked me to go down to the sandwich shop and bring back bacon, lettuce and tomato sandwiches for us. And some French fried potatoes. The hotel was called the Hollenden. We always liked to stay where the ballplayers stayed. That was where they always stayed."

John's short, declarative sentences are run-on in their sing-song rhythm, and often repetitious. "We were going to go to the ballgame that afternoon. There was going to be another game before the Indians played. An oldtimer's game. You had already bought tickets from the hotel con . . . con . . ."

"Concierge, John," Blackstone says, softly.

John sits quietly for a moment, lips moving, massaging the word. "Con-serge. Lots of very famous old time players were to be at the game. Babe Ruth and Ty Cobb and Rogers Hornsby and Jimmie Foxx and Tris Speaker and . . ."

His father gently interrupts his litany. "Please continue, John."

"Most of the tables were empty but three men were sitting at the table near where I was standing and waiting for the sandwiches and the French fried potatoes. The three men were Babe Ruth and Ty Cobb and Tris Speaker. I knew who Babe Ruth was immediately and I knew who the others were too because their pictures were in the newspaper that morning. In the Cleveland Plain Dealer." John is becoming more animated as he speaks. But then he stops, still staring into his half empty glass. He's building toward the end of his story when his eyes go glassy. His stare moves up and toward the wall opposite him. His glass tips slightly and some milk dribbles onto the rug. He does not notice. I try not to notice.

"Babe Ruth hit seven hundred and fourteen home runs and batted in two thousand two hundred and four runs and scored two thousand two hundred and seventy four times and . . . "

"John, John, please, just finish the story," says Blackstone. "My son knows more baseball statistics than perhaps anyone could ever care—or bear—to hear. He's a walking encyclopedia of the game." He nods again to John to continue.

"I had my autograph notebook and pen with me. I was very nervous but I went to the table where the men were sitting and asked if they'd sign their names for me. The others looked like I was bothering them but Mr. Ruth smiled and said to me, 'Little man, we'd be happy to give you an autograph.' That's exactly what he said. 'Little man, we'd be happy to give you an autograph.' I remember that. 'We'd be happy to give you an autograph.'" Then John stops his recitation. His mouth turns down.

"Go ahead, John," prompts his father.

"But I only had one blank page left in my autograph book. I didn't know there was only one page left." John is back in that moment, and is becoming agitated. "I always make sure there is just one autograph per page. I like it that way. But I only had one page left and . . ."

"It's all right, John."

"That's what Mr. Ruth said, too. He said it was OK and they could all sign the same page and he took it and he signed it first. Right in the middle. Then Mr. Cobb signed it." He hesitates and goes glassy-eyed again. "Ty Cobb: eight hundred and ninety two stolen bases, nineteen hundred and sixty one runs batted in, four thousand . . ."

"John!" Milton's interjection is a mild reprimand now. John again returns to the present. "Mr. Speaker signed, too. They were all on the same page. That's not the way I wanted it. And now they're gone." Then he stops again. His almost empty glass falls from his hand and he's rocking again.

He starts to cry.

There's a simian-like, wracking quality to his crying. "Babe Ruth and Ty Cobb and Tris Speaker. They're gone and I'll never see them again." He's rocking so hard now he looks like he's going to fall from his chair, and damn if he finally doesn't. Now he's writhing on the ground and sobbing. Before I can move, Thomas slips in and helps him up.

I can see that this sad and anguished sixty-something man has lost a great deal more than a set of rare autographs. I can't think of anything to say to console him. I reach for, "John, I'm sorry, you sound like you lost three of the best friends you ever had." No response. My words sound hollow. I'll just keep listening.

Blackstone wheels himself to his son, lifts his shoulders and holds his head in his lap as if John is a child again. In many ways he is. "Mr. Kent will find your Mr. Ruth and the others, John, he's just promised me that he will." That proud and stupid promise played back to me again.

John stops crying and, for the first time, looks directly at me with his spaniel eyes. "Will you, Mr. Kent? Will you bring Babe Ruth and Ty Cobb and Tris Speaker back to me?"

The plaintive question tells me precisely what the autographs mean to John Blackstone. I want to say yes, but the word sticks in my throat. Putting my hand on his shoulder I finally say, "I'll try my very best, John."

"I don't want you to merely *try*, Mr. Kent," snaps the senior Blackstone. His head wags a bit, maybe from Parkinson's, but his jaw is firmly set. "That piece of paper means more to my son than anything else in his limited world. No person— not even me —means as much. These truly have become his old friends, sir, he can't give them up. If you understand this, you'll understand why I insist that, by taking this matter upon yourself, you swear that you *will* find the autographs! In fact, sir, please further understand that your fee is contingent, not upon *trying* to find them, but only upon *finding* them. I hope I make that point *quite* clear."

The old man tends to speak in italics, and with a vehemence that wasn't in his voice earlier. In doing so he makes himself implacably clear. He must have been a formidable courtroom opponent, but right now he seems more like *my* opponent. And I don't like being talked to that way. I don't take orders to do anything. Screw the twenty-five large, He's treating me like a bounty hunter who gets nothing if he doesn't get his man. I'm ready to toss this whole impossible mess overboard. But I keep my mouth shut. Twenty-five grand is, after all, a bundle of cash. One doesn't screw twenty-five large so fast.

We wait until John recovers his self-control. Then he continues his story. The Babe must have taken a shine to him because he also gave him a pair of first row game tickets behind the Indians dugout, far better seats than the concierge's, and he invited John down to the field before the game for a photograph with him. This must have been the occasion for the smaller photo in the montage. His father had given him the concierge tickets to hold so he now gave them to some other kid in the sandwich shop, but that's all he remembers about the momentous incident.

"Please do forgive me for becoming so upset, Mr. Kent," says Blackstone, after John finishes. "Neither John nor I have been ourselves since the theft. The very thought of intruders in the house . . ."

"No problem, Mr. Blackstone." This isn't me talking, it's my prospective fee.

Blackstone beckons me to lean into him so his son can't hear. "There's something else you should know, Mr. Kent. Your success in this matter will mean every bit as much to me as to John, for more than the obvious reason. I'm ninety-one years old, sir, and my doctor has had the nerve to tell me I may not live out the year. He's just detected Pancreatic cancer, I'm afraid. On top of my damned Parkinson's."

He pauses. "I shouldn't use that word 'afraid,'" he says. "I'm not afraid of the consequences to me of my diseases. I've lived long and well, and provided fully for my son's care. But it would depress me beyond description if I were to live my remaining days with John himself in such a deep depression over this heinous theft. I want his autographs—his happiness—restored before I die. My own happiness shall return only with his. And . . ." His determination is now drifting into distraction. "And I want them returned for his mother's sake as well."

"His mother? I didn't realize . . . "

"That she's still alive? She isn't, Mr. Kent. Eve, my beloved Eve, died almost forty years ago when John was still a teen-aged boy. She was a beautiful woman, sir, inside and out. A veritable treasure. I never remarried, never could. I must tell you, she loved John dearly and somehow chose to take the blame for his condition completely upon herself, not the cruel twist of nature that it obviously was."

"She blamed herself? Why?"

"I wish she could have found an answer to that very question.

She often spoke of karma or some other such nonsense. She was born and bred in your Sausalito, you know. I believe the blame she imposed upon herself was the chief cause of her early demise. As much as anything, she died of a broken heart. Even now, I miss her more than I can say."

The old man becomes quiet now. He removes his glasses and stares into space, his eyes wet and unseeing, his mind clearly dwelling upon the past. My heart, which tends to reside on my sleeve, goes out to him. I wait till he returns from his sad reverie.

"If I appear maudlin, Mr. Kent, it's the sherry that does this to me. Though I try to avoid it, I too often seek it." I know what he means. His face softens. "The truth is, I don't like giving up old friends either. The drinking is no substitute for my Eve, but . . . Look, I'm certain you have many questions but first may I tell you of something I believe may be relevant to what has befallen us?"

I nod, ever more curious.

"John has always so enjoyed telling his story that I thought he might enjoy even more having it heard by more people. So, just recently, I asked Thomas— he's a remarkably good writer— if he could put a brief version of it on paper."

So now Thomas buttles, cooks and writes. "You'd have Thomas turn John's experience with the Babe into some kind of book or short story?"

"He's already done it, sir. Several months ago. A short story so well written that I had him submit it to National Public Radio's story-telling hour. A favorite show we listen to every weekend. NPR loved it, aired it, then recently published it in their anthology *Notes from the Past*. The book, I must tell you, is still on the New York Times Book Review best-seller list."

That hardly narrows the field, I'm thinking. "That certainly widens the suspect list," I say. "Uh, Mr. Blackstone, I guess that, through the radio show and book, millions of people have come to know that John possessed the autographs."

"Of course, Mr. Kent. That's why I'm telling you this."

Of course. My face reddens. "Well, sir, you never said this would be easy."

"True, but I'm still counting upon you to retrieve those autographs. And, if I may, sir, for their expeditious return, I will up the ante. Put the autographs in John's hands within thirty days and I'll double your fee. You have, let's see . . ." He consults a small desk calendar. ". . . till November seventeenth to complete your task. Also, I withdraw my precipitous threat to withhold your fee. But it shall be cut in half if you fail." He says this with a wan smile. Ever the wily old barrister. Then he sinks back into his wheelchair. His left hand is shaking uncontrollably. He looks totally exhausted.

But hadn't the man just asked my permission to double my fee? You may, sir, I say to myself. Obviously, the money doesn't matter to him. But for me, fifty thou is the better part of a year's earnings. A lovely motivation in itself, possibly going beyond, uh, the inspiration of the Blackstone happiness. Cynical old me. My task is set and the hour is late.

"Mr. Blackstone, my task is set and the hour is late. I thank you for your generosity and your ample hospitality. And I assure you I'll be on the case immediately and I won't stop till I've successfully concluded it." Nice speech. Well received by the look on Blackstone's face. But now I have to make myself believe what I've basically sworn to do. I say my goodbyes and am shown to the door by the doubting Thomas.

"Thomas, I'll be questioning you and others about this theft, likely tomorrow. I'm certain you won't mind, will you?"

What could he say? "Not at all, sir. I shall cooperate fully, Mr. Kent. Good evening, sir."

A lot of sir-ing going on at this "Overlook."

8.

I head back home through the Presidio. What has been elation over a huge fee dissolves into anger. Aimed squarely at me. I've allowed myself to be carried away, practically guaranteeing these fine people I'd find the autographs. Have I somehow forgotten, after all these years, that, unless you're holding a sought-after book or 'graph in your hand, you never, but never, put out a guarantee of finding it? Not about locating a fifty buck, nicely-jacketed first edition, and certainly not about a fifty gee set of sigs. It's tough enough to secure a rare sig at the right price when you know its whereabouts, but these have been stolen and I have no idea where or why they've been taken. What I do know is that this was no casual theft. Whoever snatched them knew just what he was after. Anyhow, now I've got only thirty days to prove I'm not the obvious fool I sure as hell am. I'm starting from scratch, I *literally* don't have a clue and I haven't begun to begin my investigation.

I sink a little lower into the car's seat. Well, say I to myself, think of it as any ordinary book quest. Keep it simple. Occam's Razor. But, dammit, this isn't any ordinary book, it's a unique set of rare autographs and I don't know if the thieves are trying to sell it or, like John Blackstone, keep it for themselves. And if they want to sell it, why would they risk so much for five measly grand? Christ, with all the Ming vases, or whatever other stuff is in that mansion, they could have done a lot better than swipe a bunch of sigs. But if I can answer my question—if I can just nail down the thieves' *motivation*—that would be a start to snagging ten times five grand. A nice deposit for my now-empty retirement fund.

Though it won't help my investigation, there is one thing I clearly do understand: Milton Blackstone does indeed love his son.

❏

It's near 1 a.m. when I reach the houseboat. I want to escape into a stiff nightcap, but I need to take some notes, lay a foundation. Lay out some hunches, some people to see, tickle my file of autograph houses, collectibles dealers. Like that, so I'll have a jumping-off point in the morning.

I stare at my legal pad for a solid fifteen minutes. It's a blur. Nothing comes. Not a single thought. Enough for one night. But thinking about what I've taken on wires me. A small bit of gin will clear the cobwebs and help me sleep. I pour a big bit. But worth only a small buzz. A great buzz has to be built on an empty stomach. Kent's Law.

Anyhow, while the gin is seeping in, I figure a few casts might relax me even more. And a toke or two from my dwindling stash, why not? Besides, the high tide is beginning to ebb. What with good conditions caused by the early rains this season, I might even wind up with a sturgeon.

Sturgeons are fond of ghost shrimp. I scrape up the few left in my bait can, thread them onto a swiveled double hook above a weighted leader, snap out a cast and settle back into my La-Z-Boy, promising myself I'll pack it in as soon as my glass is drained.

It's a promise I won't be able to keep.

9.

I retrieve the first cast slowly, letting the weight bounce a little on the bottom to add some action to the movement I put on the shrimp. My "fifteen minute drunk"—the real reason the martini has so many friends—is kicking in nicely. Another cast and several pullbacks to make sure I'm bottoming. Not a ripple. But, with the sixth cast, I sense a classic pumper, the familiar kiss of a sturgeon. I wait a second, then pull back an imperceptible inch. A real nibble now. A strike? I yank the line back to set it, but it goes stiff. I pull the line gently, by hand, for better feel. The slight motion seems to free it. Probably just a snag. Ain't that wonderful! A few more and I'll soon have a boatload of no fish. I laugh, leaning back, my gin rush ebbing, and I begin to reel in.

If it's a fish, I lost it. Might have lost the bait, too. I continue retrieving. Long day. Sacktime ahead.

Then, when the retrieve is just about complete, I feel another little tug. What was there still seems to be there. And whatever it is, it's hooked. Could be a largemouth. If it is, then it might's well be lookin' at a fryin' pan!

Just before I set myself to work it, the fish runs away, so fast it takes me several seconds to kill the drag, and I almost lose my grip on the rod. While it's running, I toss down the dregs of my mart, all the while convinced that . . . something serious this way comes. A large, large largemouth? Maybe even larger than a largemouth? That's OK too.

Don't take the whole line, baby, turn. *Turn, turn, turn,* I sing, just like a Byrd. If the fish hears me, it doesn't heed me. Finally, with practically nothing left on my reel, the line goes dead again. The thing is turning. It's got to be! This ain't no goddamn bass, this is typical *sturgeon* behavior. Holy jeezus, this has gotta be one big mother. Maybe a big, egg-laden female ready to make another run. Sturgeon roe tonight! I reel in, rock forward and reel in some more till I can't turn the winder. I'm working with 40-pound test line. The rod is flexed nearly to breaking, and so, almost, is my wrist. The miserable fish has to be diving now.

I hang on and pray; something I am absolutely no good at. Oh mother of God. The line relaxes once more. My fish is rising and my arms are practically falling off from pulling and speed-winding. I feel like I'm fighting a marlin off Key West.

Now's when it decides to leap. Leap, indeed, and leap it does, rising to make a perfect parabola over the surface not fifty yards away.

My lamp catches it. A stunning sight.

Doris! It has got to be goddamn *Doris*! But a sturgeon that leaps? Never mind, the bright moon tells me that it *is* Doris. It's the biggest damned sturgeon I've ever seen. Over three hundred pounds, easy, and seven feet if she's an inch. Can I hold this prehistoric monster and bring her in? I'm already near exhaustion, but I can't quit now.

More slack. More reeling in. A renewed run. Keep winding, Kent. At last the fisherman seems to be overcoming the fish. Twice, Doris is within gaffing distance. But how am I going to handle the gaff *and* the rod? I sure as hell can't net her. I need a couple more hands—deckhands, actually—and a net the size of a hot tub. And she can make another run anytime. Christ, if she does, I'm gonna need a seatbelt on my La-Z-Boy.

❏

I've been at this for over an hour. I'm drenched with sweat. My concern for my fat paycheck is forgotten. My back is breaking, but I'm coaxing Doris closer. She's visibly running out of steam. So am I.

She's now only twenty yards away and seems about ready for the gaff. She's putting me in mind of a huge, iced bowl of caviar sitting next to a jeroboam of chilled Veuve Cliquot. "Come to papa, baby, come to papa, do!" I sing-shout. Out loud. Very loud.

The old girl can easily turn again while I'm readying the tethered gaff, but she seems to have forgotten her ancient instincts. She pauses, I guess for a consult with her pea-sized brain. Then she makes what she must understand will be her last run ever.

Come to papa? It's as though Doris has actually heard me. She turns a few degrees more and—guided by what?—locks herself onto a laser path directly at my lounger like she has something personal against me. I freeze for a second. When I finally realize what's happening, I snap my rig into its holster and snatch blindly at the gaffing pike.

I get a real sense that old Doris is signaling some kind of a last testament, a final word. Moving with all the speed she can gather, she makes a demented leap—that uncharacteristic leap again—that launches her into a high arc over the aft railing and straight down toward me. Can a sturgeon do that? Is this really happening? Me, I'm standing here like Captain Ahab, my gaff raised and ready to strike.

I let loose my lethal weapon, not to snag the possessed beast but suddenly to protect myself from her. The gaff, poorly propelled, splashes harmlessly in the bay.

But Doris, bless her, doesn't land so harmlessly. She comes crashing down on top of me, flipping me backwards over my lounger, slamming my head into the bulkhead and knocking me cold for a few seconds. Or minutes. How would I know? When I come to, I find myself lying flat out on the deck, my head split open and bleeding, and my arms hugging the old girl who's now looking at me, her big, defiant eyes expressing the indignation of a spurned lover.

I can't take in the enormity of what has just taken place. I've somehow landed my quarry—or been landed by her—but the battle isn't over yet. Doris is weak from her struggle, but more so now for lack of life-giving water. Still, she's very much alive. For a long moment her sad, clouding eyes are locked on my glassy ones in a mortal stare-down. I have to make a quick decision. Take care of my head or take Doris down.

The head can get fixed. I'm not about to lose this leviathan.

❏

I try to forget the growing ache in my skull. I'd feel a lot worse if I weren't feeling so damned euphoric about landing—decking— this distinguished lady. Lying next to me, she looks exquisite, even in her primeval ugliness. All I have to do is hang onto her. A few minutes more and she'll succumb. At last, Doris's wriggling death throes begin to subside.

There's blood flowing into my eyes. My headache is growing, but I force myself to relax. I even let a daydream in. There's the lovely Doris, stuffed, mouth open, barbels rampant, hanging in a diving position from the vaulted ceiling of my library/shop. No, it's not my library/shop, it's the Ovid Kent Sturgeon Room of the Smithsonian Institution, the site created to honor the holder of the world's record for white sturgeon, the prize fish being taken in the Bay of . . ."

10.

"Let her go."

"What!" say I, jerked out of my reverie by a gruff voice.

"You heard me. I said let her go. Send her back. Do it now."

The nascent moon has disappeared. By the dim light from the cabin, I can make out only that the insistently barked orders are coming from a large, bulky man sitting slumped back in the director chair next to my lounger. Am I hallucinating? He's wearing a long camel hair overcoat and a matching newsboy cap pulled low over his eyes. Staring straight ahead, he's smoking a cigar, blowing perfect smoke rings, one through the other. He repeats his demand that I return my prize to the deep.

I've never met the man but I know who he is. Immediately.

Without hesitating, I release my hold on the old gal, pull out my skinning knife from the side of the lounger and cut the line. Bracing myself against the bulkhead, I use my legs and the rest of my waning strength to shove the barely-moving Doris over the side and into the waiting bay. She barely fits under the lower rung of my rear rail.

Quickly reviving, she remains near the surface, swims a few yards out, turns and—I swear it—rises and looks directly back at me. To mock me? To thank me? Or to thank this stranger who would become a stranger to me no more? A few seconds later she dives to the bottom of the bay, never, I am certain, to pass her deceived lips over a passing lure again.

I sigh. My head is splitting, my face covered with blood. I turn to look into the beady eyes of the big man in the camel hair coat.

11.

"Why did you make me do that?" I say.

It seems a logical question. But I find myself asking it of George Herman "Babe" Ruth. The Babe. The Bambino. The Sultan of Swat. The greatest goddamn ball player who ever lived. I must be hallucinating. It can't be the gin. Its effects were obliterated by my battle-induced rush of adrenalin. I *gotta* be hallucinating.

The hour is late, the pain is strong, the blow had been to my head. But no, this has to be The Man Himself. In what appears to be the flesh. In this dim light it's hard to tell. If it isn't him, it's a damned good facsimile. I'm tempted to reach out and touch him to settle my curiosity, but my awe saps my resolve. My heart is still pounding at the excitement of landing—and losing—old Doris, but I'm not even thinking of her now. I can only think that, out of nowhere—well, maybe out of this new task I've accepted —I'm face to face with the most famous athlete in history. Georgerhermanbaberuth.

"Because you've got better things to do. More important things," says the Babe, evenly, in the pinch-mouthed style familiar to me from the old newsreels. He takes another deep puff of his cigar. "And, by the way, kid, I didn't *ask* you to dump her, did you notice? I *demanded* you do it. If I was a little rough on you, I'm sorry." All this while he hasn't even looked at me, just at his smoke rings breaking up against my rear railing.

There are a million questions I want to ask Georgeherman-baberuth. None have anything to do with fishing. The first is a single word because I just can't get my mind in gear. "Why?"

He blows another ring, looks at me for the first time and grins. "I just told you. You got better things to do."

"No, Mr . . . Mr. Ruth? That's not what I mean. You are Babe Ruth, aren't you?

"Yep."

"I'm asking why are you here? *How* are you here? *Are* you here?" I'm speaking in italics, like Blackstone. "What's going *on* here?"

"Hey, kid, call me Babe," he grins. I know this huge, close-mouthed grin. Millions and millions of people do. "Everyone calls me that. Everyone where I come—came—from. First, I should tell you I'm no game warden. I'm not here about your fish."

I hardly thought so. This switch to geniality is dissolving my awe. "Look, Mr. . . . Babe, I'm a little confused. A whole lot confused. It's late, I'm exhausted, I hurt bad, my skull's been split open and I may have a concussion, so I'm not sure what I'm saying *or* seeing right now. Is it really you talking to me? Are you really here or am I talking to myself? Right at the moment—I'm not kidding, Babe—I don't know if I'm awake or dreaming."

"Relax. It's me, kid. I'm here, even if my body isn't, which it isn't. The explanation gets a little complicated, but get used to me because I'll be hanging with you for as long as it takes to get you where you're trying to go with this little problem of yours. That's the way it was set up. For me, for us."

"For you? For *us*? Set up by who?"

"The Boss." The Babe says this like I should know who he's talking about. I have an inkling. "And I wouldn't be a straight-shooter if I didn't tell you why He assigned me to you." I can hear the capitals in his "Boss" and his "He."

My eyes are riveted on the Babe's pudgy face. "You sure you got the right guy?"

"You sure you're Ovid Kent? Anyhow, it's about my old, brief connection with the Blackstone kid. That should come as no surprise to you.

"No, Babe, why should I be the least bit sur—"

But he cuts off my attempt at sarcasm with another shocker. "It's also about your mother."

"My mother?" I'm stunned. "What's she got to do with—"

He cuts me off again. "The Boss, in his inimitable way, happens to know that while you had a mother, you sort of didn't have one, OK? She left you and your dad when you were still a young kid."

Tell me something I don't know, Babe. I loved my mother for hooking me on books and making me stretch my mind and my experience. But I hate her even more for . . . Why am I defending myself? My mind's in a turmoil, boggled by the collision of the long day's events and the collision of my head with my bulkhead. But I remain focused on this singular man who does not appear to be going away.

The Bambino goes on. "Y'now, kid, if I were chosen to drop in on the Blackstone kid, he'd never question my being there. Anyhow, as you may know, my mother disappeared, too. I was an orphan. Born in Baltimore. Never had a mother or father I knew of. The Boss, He's a sympathetic guy—merciful, they say—so, seeing as you're looking for these missing autographs, mine included, and also that the three of us—you, me and John Blackstone—were without mothers all or most of our lives, He musta tied all this stuff together and . . . here I am. He works in mysterious ways, I guess you knew that."

It takes me a while to absorb all this before I can speak. "That's why you're here? I can use all the help . . ." I stop myself from reciting clichés to Babe Ruth. "Look, Babe, I still don't understand it, but I do feel honored. You are here, I buy that. But where do we go *from* here?"

"That's up to you. Let me ask you a question about this case of ours." I like the way he says "ours." "You think you can find the autographs, kid?"

"Yes, Babe, I think I can."

"You think you can or you know you can?" he shoots back.

Where is he going with this? He's making me feel as uncomfortable as Milton Blackstone had. No fooling this guy. Real or not, the Bambino ain't goin' away. "OK, I *don't* know, Babe, that's what I should have said. I just don't know. I was impressed by Milton Blackstone's offer and was moved by John Blackstone's predicament so I shot my big mouth off and promised to find his son's precious autographs, that's the truth of it. Fact is, though, I just don't know if I can find those sigs. So what do I do now?"

"Keep talkin' straight like that, kid, same as I talk with you. If you do, I may be able to help you. I don't know who stole the autographs either, but, what the hell, I'm on your side. By the way, you deserve to know that the Boss has something in it for me, too."

"That's good. I'm glad you're aboard, Babe." In spite of my miserable headache, I remember to offer him a drink. He turns it down. The Bambino turning down a drink?

"Love one. A real one. Real cigar, too, and a real woman and a whole lot more. But I'd have to 'break the wall'—materialize— to do it. I can't though because I'm only a Level Three Proto. I have to settle for Proto Three scotch and cigars. Which taste like Four Roses and Rum Soaked Crooks. Which is to say they taste like crap—like thin air, which is what they are, and which, at the moment, is what I am, but there's nothing I can do about it. I can advise you, but I can't do for you. Not in this state anyhow. Not now, not yet."

"Not now, not yet?"

"Maybe if we find what we're lookin' for, the Boss might kick me up a notch or two where the perks are better. That's what I meant by 'something in it for me.' A little single malt scotch, a

Havana Montecristo, even a lousy hot dog; they'd taste great right about now. I hope you're getting all this."

Sidetracked again, and fascinated, I shake my head trying to shunt the Babe's meanderings into my overflowing brainpan. I'm not sure what I'm getting. This "proto" man likes to talk and probably hasn't had a chance to do so with a real person in years, or maybe ever since he left us in 1948. My pain is ramping up and I'm still bleeding, but this is Babe Ruth, so let him talk all night. I guess I'll take all this insanity on faith alone.

"I hope you do, kid."

Was I talking out loud?

"Hey, you look awful. Get yourself to a hospital. I gotta go now."

"Will I see you again soon?"

"Yeah."

"When?"

"When you're supposed to."

"One last thing, Babe?"

"What's that?"

"If we're going to be working together, would you mind calling me Ovid?"

"Sure, kid. And, by the way, Mr. Fisherman, you should know that old Doris couldn't leap like that again if she tried. But she did it to hook up with you, so are you still wondering if *we're* supposed to hook up?"

And with three more words—"Purpose to everything"—the Sultan of Swat's ethereal image slowly evaporates into the thick Headlands fog now making its seasonal assault on the Bay.

12.

I drag myself to my office, staggering, tripping as usual, then swearing. Never will get used to these high nautical thresholds. As I sit, still dazed, my mind wanders to my book stacks. I walk among them and run my hand over my full sets of Sinclair Lewis, Maugham, Sax Rohmer, and Cronin, many signed. Complete 19th and 20th Century oeuvres are my specialty, autographs a sideline. James Jones, Jules Verne, C.S. Forester, Hilton, Trollope. I don't just collect and sell them. I've read them. Many, twice or more. I've come to love them almost too much to sell them.

A twinge of pain yanks me back to my aching present.

I stumble into the head, toss up my gin and prime rib, then gargle some Lavoris and toss down a handful of aspirin and an Alka Seltzer. It's well past 5 a.m. and the first rays of daylight are limning the Bay Bridge. As I wait for the pills to kick in, I stare at the bloody, unshaven face that stares back at me in my mirror. It's a lived-in face fronting a craggy, cleft-chinned skull that's almost too big for its barely-six-foot frame. Thick mustache. Thick, 96-bright white hair. Jowls waiting to jump out. An acceptable package, if not at the moment. Even if it takes a thirty-eight inch belt to wrap it.

The headache isn't going away. And with it I have the oddest feeling that, though this may be the longest day of my life, it's still got a long way to go.

Am I really going to be partnering with *Babe Ruth*? Am I actually going to see the Bambino again? The daylight will tell me what's real; the Babe, the booze or the bonk on the head. He was right about the hospital. I have to get there right away. I wash off most of the caked blood on my face, drape a wet hand towel over my head, jam on an ancient Cleveland Indians cap and, looking like a Jewish Lawrence of Arabia, take off for Marin General, just up 101 in Kentfield, speeding all the way, almost hoping a cop will stop me. Hell, what a lovely story I'd have to tell.

But he'd never believe it.

13.

After a forty minute wait—even at this ridiculous hour—in ER Reception, I'm fighting my impatient anger more than my pain. But then I find myself in a wheelchair, about to tell my woes to a disconcertingly beautiful angel of mercy. Triage may be her vocation, but, from my first glance of her standing in front of the high-wattage X-ray readers across from the intake room, she could easily be a Broadway chorine. Behave, Kent, you may still be hallucinating. *If* you're hallucinating.

Though she's wearing a sort of uniform—clunky white shoes, white stockings, a long skirt and a faded blue cardigan sweater—the high lumens from the light boxes clearly tell me just how perfect her long legs are. The kind Florenz Ziegfeld demanded for his Follies, the kind that can hold a silver dollar between their possessor's knees, calves and ankles all at once. I saw that once in an AMC movie. I have difficulty lifting my prying eyes up to her face, but it's worth it when I do.

Her eyes, framed by black-rimmed glasses, are fixed on a medical chart. From her laugh lines I take her to be in her early forties. She has a delicious fullness to her upper lip and a noble, almost aquiline nose. Her hair, a mix of blond and brown, is carelessly clamped into a bun, its color looking natural, but how would I know? What I do observe is that she's not wearing a wedding band.

Intelligent. No-nonsense, yet easygoing. Sensuous. Great sense of humor. While waiting I'm generating a fabulous persona for her, and an interesting scenario for the two of us as she walks in and sits down in front of me, putting an abrupt end to my ogling fantasy. From behind her desk, and without looking up from her clipboard, she tells me who I am.

"Ovid Kent, possible concussion," says she, possessor of the silver dollar legs. Her voice, though all business, comes off as low and sexy. Precisely as predicted.

I'm feeling totally goofy by now, made so either by what I've been through or by serious sleep deprivation or the very presence of her. I correct her. "I'm Ovid Kent, possible broken heart."

She glances at me for the first time, ignoring my remark and quickly looking back at her clipboard. A reprimand is on her lovely face. "Mr. Kent, can you tell me, please—briefly if possible —what brought you here this morning?"

"My PT Cruiser." Feeble. But, even if I'm hurting, I'm desperate to put a smile on those bursting lips.

She stares at me now, her huge brown eyes blinking, her gorgeous lips compressed.

"OK, OK, I'll behave."

"Thank you, Mr. Kent. Now, what happened to you?"

"I've fallen. In love."

Her eyes roll. She lays the clipboard on her desk then places her hands, palms down, on it. "How droll, Mr. Kent. But, wherever you think you're going with your snappy repartee, you're not. I've had a long, hard night and you look like you have, too, so I must ask you to answer my questions in a straightforward manner or I'll send you back to the waiting room where others, perhaps more needy of our care than you, are waiting."

"A fish caught me." I'm taking a chance here of being booted out altogether, but at least I'm telling the truth.

A smile shows through. Not sincere. "You're done here, Mr. Kent!"

What is wrong with me? I actually slap myself on the cheek.

But, before she can see how phony a move this is, I offer, "I'm sorry, miss, I really am sorry." Before she can react I blurt out the short version of what she's asked of me, my strange lunker sturgeon fishing tale. Minus the Babe, of course.

By now, my head is throbbing and the pain is traveling to my shoulders. Shock? The room begins a slow spin. I'm looking at six of her beautiful faces trying to figure out which is the real one.

She looks at my only one and asks, "This all took place at your home?"

"What? Oh. Yes. Home and office. Houseboat. Sausalito." Her full, natural brows move up a bare fraction of an inch. She appears to see me for the first time. "Did I say something odd?" I ask.

"No," replies Nurse Knight. Knight is the name on the badge that rests above the hard-to-ignore swell of her cardigan. "I live just up from Sausalito in a houseboat, too," She, almost invisibly, shakes off her apparently regrettable, off-subject response. "I have a few more questions before an emergency doctor can see you."

She'd let a personal fact slip through. Has my story punctured a tiny hole in her wall of resistance? Am I being optimistic? Yes. But I'm glad I haven't cracked wise again, idiot I've become. Or am. A lot of questions follow. DOB, previous hospitalizations, allergies, medications, family history of diseases. Nurse Knight is only doing her job, but I convince myself she's forging ahead because she doesn't want to give me a conversational foothold.

Can't blame her.

I'd love a martini right now. But why am I thinking of this at six in the morning? Not thinking straight. And why, I ask myself, am I acting like a love-starved schoolboy? Only half of that is true.

"May I ask your first name?" I ask. Nurse Knight is an RN. She must understand I'm in agony with a likely dangerous condition that requires quick intervention, so she's in-taking me fast for my sake, not just to get rid of the bozo I've been. This is what

I want to believe. I'm hoping she's at least a little impressed by my ability to keep up this nifty lounge-lizard patter while fighting pain and dizziness that's growing stronger every minute.

"You may ask," she replies. This is her complete answer. Then she goes back to her writing as I gaze at her exquisite face.

He's not a bad-looking sort, she's thinking. He's more of a chunk than a hunk, a little over the hill. Kind of looks like he's been hanging out under a bridge. Probably drinks from a bagged bottle. A good face though. Lived in. What more must I know to convince myself of his basic goodness? What's the best way to learn who this deep and delicious man is? By sleeping with him, of course. And, by the way, I believe that I am, in spite of myself, truly and deeply in love him.

I shelve this latest fantasy. I mean to return to it as soon as I've pocketed Blackstone's fifty grand. The mere thought of him and the task he's assigned me makes me wince. I was supposed to be at Overlook today to begin my investigation.

Oy.

Now even my digression has digressed. "Nurse Knight, you were going to tell me your name?"

"Florence. The 'Knight' is short for 'Nightingale.'" She says this with a perfectly straight face.

She's yanking my string. But haven't I been yanking hers? "Nightingale is not your real name, is it?"

"No, Mr. Kent. Is Ovid yours?"

"No, it isn't," I reply. "It's Clark. Clark Kent. I'm Superman, but please keep that to yourself, Lois. Actually, my name really *is* Ovid." I want to explain my real connection to the "real" Clark Kent, but my head, not hers, is now demanding all my attention. It's ready to split into three parts. *Kentus patum est divisa in partes tres.*

All business again, she wheels me into an examining cubicle. It's after 6 a.m. I haven't slept in nearly twenty-four hours, I'm exhausted and my headache is getting a headache. But the exam, the MRI and the stitches happen quickly, and soon I'm in a darkened private room, my head swathed in bandages, an IV in my arm and my pain removed by a heavy dose of what must be Vicodin.

Though my mind is shutting down, I remember that Nurse Knight never told me her first name. Her real first name.

❏

The door opens to let in a spike of light. An angel wafts through and morphs into Babe Ruth.

"Is that you, Babe?" I mumble, my eyes unfocused.

"Still trying, aren't you, Mr. Kent?" replies Nurse Knight.

It's her! Barely awake now, I reach for some extemporaneous poetry. "Wounded though I be, lying here on this field of battle —"

"*Babble* is more like it. I don't want you talking, I want you to get some rest. The floor nurse tells me you can't sleep, so he's given me something to sedate you.

"Seduce me?"

"You are delirious, aren't you? I look in on all my intakes before I go off duty. Even my naughty ones. She stabs a sedative into my IV line.

I'm about out again. "Hey, Miz Nightingale," I mumble, "you never tol' me your first name."

"It's Karen," she replies softly. "Go back to sleep, Mr. Kent."

"Will I see you again?" If she gives me an answer, I'm not awake to hear it.

But then—a minute later, an hour?—I see her staring at me. I'm dreaming. Or am I?

She smiles, fixes my head bandage, bends over me, then does something odd. Very, extremely odd. She drops a touch of a kiss on my forehead and whispers into my ear, "I don't do *that* for any of my patients." I swear this is exactly what she does and exactly what she says. Well, I think so.

She slips out of the room. Out of my life as well? Was that a goodbye kiss? Was it a kiss? Did it even happen? Did Knight happen? Did the Babe happen? What the hell *did* happen? What the hell is going on?

14.

I'm awakened by a male nurse and a dull throbbing in my temples. I stare in disbelief at the wall clock. It's hardly moved! But the guy informs me I've slept a dozen hours straight. Still, I vaguely remember being wakened once to be medicated or something.

"Morning, Mr. Kent, I'm Pete, your nurse. Time to take a snapshot of your head. If it checks out, you can do the same, soon as the doc sees you. Here at Marin General, we fix 'em, then we kicks 'em. Out."

"Is Karen Knight on duty today?" Karen? Where did that come from?

Pete smiles knowingly. "Naw, Karen left for Acapulco."

I guess I got her name right. "C'mon, Pete, is she here?" He's a wise guy, like me. Don't like him already.

"My friend, I got no idea where she is. Nobody else does either. Seems most every male patient she's ever attended asks me that. A few women, too. She's not married, but whatever you got in mind, forget it. Karen Knight is the most private person I've ever known. I don't know where she lives, who she dates, *if* she dates, nothing about her except, even though she's pretty new here, she's probably the best damned RN in the joint. You ready to roll?"

❏

My "snapshot" approved—it was a mild concussion—I'm home within the hour where I collapse then awaken at four and make a nice frosted martini followed by some defrosted shrimp and a three-day-old apple fritter. Don't usually have a mart this early in the day but I've got a day to make up for. The drink is for the throbbing in my head but it doesn't sit too well with the meds in my belly. Five minutes later, the whole works goes overboard. Damn, I hate to waste good gin.

Depression starts to seep under my stitches. My cupboard of luck is as bare as my ever-empty fridge. I'm now certain that the Babe was a Doris-induced hallucination. Maybe the whole Doris thing was, too. Maybe I just had a drunken fall. If the Bambino was for real, I'd appreciate even a bunt from him right now. The head is still killing me and I have a four week—less than four week—deadline attached to a fat fee, but a slim chance of ever earning it. Hell, my not showing up the next day at, whatever it's called, Overlook, might mean I've already blown the whole wad. Easy come, easy go. Hah! And I've got no idea if I'll ever again see the intake angel who's taken over my mind. She, for sure, was real. But everything in my life right now is a question. And no answers are in sight, and damn, this headache will not go away.

I do my threshold dance into the head and stare at myself for a second. No prettier a sight than the day before. Or was it the day before that? My beard makes me look sinister, like something left over from a Burning Man Festival. And I smell bad. Tomorrow will be a better day. It can't be worse than the 30-hour day I've just been through.

15.

The next morning's bay fog matches the state of my mind. My normally semi-jolly wake-up mood isn't materializing. Neither is my great, good friend, Mr. Ruth. I've got a lot to do, starting with a call to Milton Blackstone to explain my late start on the search. But, first things first, I'll strip my head bandage, tie a plastic bag over my head and take my worthless life. Nah, I'll just take a shave and an endless shower. Looking in the mirror, I remove the clip and begin to unwrap the bandage.

Which is when I see it. In the mirror.

Tiny numbers in reverse, neatly block-printed, covered up by the end of the cloth. Ten numbers, no name, nothing else. I peel off the rest of the bandage, reach for my specs and jot the numbers down. Karen's phone number. Nurse Karen Knight's personal and private telephone number. It has to be. But can it be? Suddenly, I'm feeling better.

Very much better.

Was I asleep when she wrote it? Was I dreaming about her take on me? She doesn't want to start something in the hospital so she secretly writes her number where I won't see it till I get home. I wish. But what if someone else . . . yeah, that damned nurse, Pete. What if he wrote the number? A prank from a first-class prankster. He said he didn't know her number. That I believe. Oh, Christ, maybe it's *his* number. Why the hell am I

50

sitting here talking to myself? *Call the goddamn number*!

I carefully—very carefully—punch up the magic digits. One ring. Two. Don't get your hopes up, old boy. Too late, they already are. A third ring. Hang up. No, let it keep ringing. What if it's a voicemail? What'll I say? A fourth ring. A fifth.

Then a pick-up.

It's Karen's beautiful, deep-throated voice, not Pete's. I exhale. Has she been waiting for this call? Who gives a damn. She answered it. "How's your busted head, Superman?" Caller ID.

As usual, I start talking before I start thinking. "This is not Superman, ma'am. This is a slightly asthmatic, slightly overweight, late baby boomer of the Jewish faith, never wed and presently unattached and therefore available for outings or other purposes." This is Kent's way. Put it all up front. Throws 'em off guard. This is the entire distillation of my thinking about the acquiring of women. It may say something about the fact that I am not with one now nor have I been lately. But, whatever else it is, it is the Credo of Kent. What's needed now is a simple invitation.

"Care to share a pizza?" Perhaps this is too simple.

"Yes," says Karen."

Simple question, simple answer. Good answer. Excellent answer. What else can I say to move us forward? "I don't like anchovies, do you?"

"No."

"You know what that means?"

"I think so. We don't like anchovies."

I like her vein of humor. I decide to push my luck. "What time can you be here?"

"You're pushing your luck, Mr. Kent," she confirms. But the last time she said "Mr. Kent" it didn't sound this forgiving.

"Does that mean you'll be here?" No immediate answer. "If I drive in this debilitated condition, Nurse Knight, I could have a cerebral hemorrhage, crash and die a horrible flaming death."

"How convincing. Where's *here*?"

I give Karen the directions. Her place, I'm not unhappy to learn, is practically around the corner. Gourmet pizza for two. I'll order, she'll pick it up, I'll pay her back, one o'clock this afternoon. She says she'll be here. Karen Knight will be here.

I haven't felt this giddy since my junior prom at Cleveland Heights High. Ms. Karen Knight is bringing her spectacular self to lunch this very day at Mr. Ovid Kent's floating domicile. Oh. Glorious. Day. Who says you can't get away with smartass?

I grab the phone and ring up Milton Blackstone. He takes his good old time getting to it and sounds reserved, almost angry. No surprise. I spill out my story and he says he understands, but he sounds skeptical. I arrange to be there at eleven the next morning to explain (lie about) my undue diligence.

Today belongs to my triage nurse.

I grab two trash bags. The first I stuff with the detritus of bachelor living. The second I stuff with the same.

In the shower, my *Old Man River* never comes out with better resonance. "*Body's all achin' and wracked with pain . . .*" Not any more! My wobbly baritone soon invites a familiar tympani accompaniment; the clunk of empty beer cans thrown at my permanently anchored vessel by my treasured eighty-one-year-old neighbor, Ethel.

"Thanks for the affirmation, Ethel," I holler. I segue into *It's a lovely day today*. Out of ammunition, she can only shout, "Hey, Ov, you in love again?"

"You finished recycling, Mrs. Witherspoon? Since you choose to be so nosy, good lady, the answer is yes, I believe I am in love again. And for once it's with someone besides you." I feel like telling Ethel. I feel like telling the world.

Peering from her galley, which faces my houseboat, she must notice my freshly self-bandaged pate. "Let me guess, Ovid. You broke your thick skull, went to the hospital and fell in love with your nurse."

I have to tell her she's right. Isn't much gets past Ethel

Witherspoon. I do love this wise and remarkable woman.

"You OK? How'd it happen? Never mind about the accident, what about the nurse?"

"You're all heart, Ethel." I give her a synopsis, again without the Babe.

"I'll give you till your stitches come out before you forget her name . . . if you ever remembered to get it. As if she'd remember the likes of you past the hospital door."

I love my Ethel. Did I say that? Ethel Witherspoon was a West Virginia librarian now long into her retirement. She's the acknowledged queen of the pier, unofficial Welcome Wagon lady and the first to circulate "Save the Houseboats" petitions whenever developers attempt to gentrify the funky nauticality of the neighborhood. She's also the most intuitive woman I've ever met.

Ethel is, however, as lousy a cook as me. But we love to grill our burgers or the fish we're both so good at catching. After a typical so-so meal, we wind up sipping a few beers or more of an evening and swapping lies or talking about the books and authors we most revere. We use each other's well-laden bookshelves as lending libraries. I'd trust her with a Gutenberg first.

Ethel's the mother I wish I'd had. But that's another story. Is Ethel right? Maybe I am flying too high. As the thought comes, another relentless fog bank wells up from the headlands. I'm hit by an involuntary shiver. "I'll let you know how things go," I say, less perky than before. "Over a beer. Soon. I promise."

"Suit yourself, Kent. But watch yourself, too."

"Yeah, I'll watch myself," I hear myself saying, as I slide my window shut. Watching myself? Never been much good at that. Easy to happen when no one's watching over you.

Oh, shut up, Kent. Count your one o'clock blessing.

❏

"She's putting out good advice." This from the Babe, who steps out of the fog. Into my cabin. "Hey, kid, glad to see you in one piece again." He's smoking his ubiquitous stogie and wearing the camel hair coat and cap, but, though it's a warm day, he looks considerably more comfortable than me. Much as I need the Babe's help, I'm not too happy with his timing. Karen's due shortly. It's like your mother dropping into the seat next to you on your first date at the movies.

"Good to see *you*, Babe." I'm already feeling easy enough with him to lie.

"Came by to compliment your taste," he says. "Your woman's a real looker, but . . ."

"But . . .?" I should know better, but I'm ticked at the Babe's knowing about Karen.

"But you got to remember, you—*we*—got a job to do. Not much time left to do it."

"Now hold on just one minute, Babe. You may be right but I don't particularly appreciate your interest in my personal life. Afraid it makes you come off as a, a peeping Tom. Are you able to do that any time you feel like it?"

"Yep," he says, scowling his annoyance at my remark, "it's part of my celestial privileges, kid." He taps a two-inch ash that disappears before it hits the floor. "But in your case it's my duty too, so don't get so outta whack. I don't care what you do when you're not working, but I do need to see some movement here. In a month I'll be totally wrapped up in full-time negotiations for Pete Rose's future and . . ."

"You can help Pete Rose with the Hall of Fame?"

"No, no, no, kid, I mean his *ultimate* future." He's smiling now.

The Babe's remark loosens me a little. "So you think Karen is pretty, huh, Babe?"

"A real angel. Which I'm sure she'll be some day. More'n I can say for you."

"Can I tell her what you said?"

"That's up to you," he winks. He was known for his wink in his day. Used it on the kids, used it on the ladies. "Anyhow, try to put your 'courtship' aside so we can get busy, huh? I speak for the . . ."

"Boss, right?"

"Right," he says. "I'll get back to you when you're ready to get back to work. Which had better be soon, real soon." With that, he's gone.

Ethel. Blackstone. The Babe. "Can I have a private moment here?" I look up and ask, out loud. Out of a now-clear sky it starts to pour, then stops in exactly ten seconds. "Same to you," I say.

No one's going to take this day away from me. No one. Not even Him.

16.

Minutes later, I'm watching Karen, the sharp breeze making her hair fly behind her, wheel her mint Miata into my parking lot. She gracefully unfolds from it, hoists the fourteen-inch everything-but-anchovies, and walks over to me. I stand helpless, staring at the vision of her, my mouth half open. This is how a woman is supposed to look, supposed to walk. She sees me staring, laughs and burlesques the way she thinks I prefer a woman to look and walk. I take a deep breath. A gulp, actually. I even forget to hold in my gut. She's wearing tight jeans, a heavy, black turtleneck pullover and plain white Keds.

Keds. I always thought Keds were for kids. She don't look like no kid.

Her smile, when she notices we're wearing practically identical outfits, lights up her comely face. Mine, too. She stops in front of me. Neither of us says a word. We just look at each other for an hour. Karen is the first to speak.

"You'll be happy to take this very heavy pizza but in your debilitated condition you might stagger and fall and die a horrible flaming death." A stern look goes along with her words. Followed by a musical laugh. My face goes red.

Competing for the sausage slices, we eat the whole damned pizza, washing it down with a superior Duckhorn cab I'd been saving for a hopeful New Year's tete-a-tete . . . who? After half an hour of small talk, I'm ready to tell Karen my entire life story, but I suppress the urge. I've gone there too early, too often before. Men like to talk about themselves, but women like their men a little mysterious. A woman also likes a man who likes to talk about her. These are facts. I'm pretty sure about them.

"Tell me about you," I say.

And soon, with the Duckhorn working, she does tell me about herself. Is she as hungry as me for someone to talk with? She goes on for another twenty minutes, non-stop. I want to interrupt her delicious little stories to match them with mine. A terrible habit. But I manage to keep my mouth shut and listen. Which is a new thing with me.

❏

Karen—nee Koscinski—is the much older sister of two brothers. Born in Merriam, a poor town just outside of Kansas City, Missouri, she lost her mother to alcohol before she reached her teens. Her oblivious father owned a struggling used car lot called *Harry's Cherries*. After her mother died, he brought home, without consulting Karen, a series of women who mostly ignored her. Karen had to fend for herself and her brothers. When her father finally remarried, it was to someone not much older than her, a mean-spirited woman who saw her only as a rival for his affections. That's when Karen decided to move on. Had to move on.

In her mid-twenties, she became a Las Vegas dancer. The big costumes, the big hair, the six-inch platforms, the push-up bras, the whole bit. Even with two left feet, she held down spots in lounge acts, first at the Desert Inn then at several other Strip hotels. After too many wrong turns on stage, and too many wrong guys off, she found herself waitressing back at the very DI lounge where she'd once danced. She made more money toting cocktails than she ever did hoofing.

Five years later she met an older guy, Danny Knight, a casino boss whose connections wangled him a point in the DI operation. She never asked questions. She liked the guy and wasn't put off by his appearing to have a lot more money than his position seemed to warrant. She didn't ask questions.

For a short while, they were happy together. But he didn't want the baby she deeply longed for. After a year, April came along. Knight was upset and accused her of defying him by not using birth control. Though she never admitted it, his accusation was justified.

After that, things completely fell apart. Danny did a lot of coke and drank a lot like her mother had. And there were other women like her father always had. She put up with this for a year, then got fed up with the way he no longer denied, but flaunted his affairs. When she filed for divorce, he became enraged. He finally caved, though, but not before giving her a black eye, then a shopping bag full of fifties. This, after she swore she'd have him arrested for what he did to her and for what she knew about him. Extortion? A small crime, compared. When he told her she was through in Vegas and had damn well better clear out, she didn't need his encouragement. She left.

What Knight didn't give her, however, was April. He didn't want his daughter but was willing to use her custody as revenge for Karen even thinking about having him arrested. Karen spent most of the money he'd given her fighting him in court. He claimed she was a lousy mother and some of this—though she fought the idea—she allowed herself to believe. So she backed down and put her fight for April on hold. She was heartbroken but figured—stupidly, she came to realize—that Knight's money would give April a better life than she could.

She wound up alone in San Francisco, stuffed her remaining cash into a no-load mutual fund, got a job in a diner while attending nursing school, and lived in a fourth floor walk-up in the Mission. She never quite figured out what the hell had hit her.

Then a miracle happened.

She got word from the domestic court in Vegas that Danny had been arrested for rigging roulette wheels and for money laundering, and would she mind picking up her daughter, she'd been awarded April's custody.

Karen was getting a chance to rectify the worst mistake she'd ever made.

Long story short, she collected April, collected her RN and settled in to her converted tugboat docked on Richardson Bay.

I can hardly believe she's telling me all this but I'm deeply moved that she is. I can't remember wanting to listen to any woman more than I want to listen to this woman.

The Blackstones can wait.

She must notice how I'm looking at her. She tells me she's not used to a man with such open ears. But I'm thinking how badly hurt she's been by men she *thought* had open ears. Thanks for listening," she says. Then: "Here I go again, thinking high-minded thoughts about a guy I've just met. I've done that too often. Made the same mistakes over and over. That's the definition of . . ."

"Insanity. I know. I've made 'em, too. So how big a deal would it be for you, for me, too, to make another with each other?"

There comes the smile again. "You've actually listened to this run-on narrative. It's not my style at all. At work they call me 'The Sphinx'. Look at us. Two fools in the fog, pumped up with pizza and just yakkin' away." But she doesn't apologize for monopolizing the conversation. Nor need she.

She kisses me instead. *She* kisses *me*. For no reason at all. Or for the best of reasons. It's a light, leaning-over, just-touching kiss. But on the mouth, not the forehead.

I take her hand and pull her, ever so gently, to my cabin, never taking my eyes off her irresistible face. We don't speak. At the bedroom door, I turn, continue to look at her longingly and scoop her up into my arms. The wedding night without the wedding. Returning my gaze and smiling an inscrutable smile, she doesn't resist. Without looking, I attempt to negotiate the threshold.

The negotiation falls apart.

The goddamn wall of the goddamn threshold reaches up and grabs my goddamn foot. The bed breaks both our fall and our mood as we wind up bouncing off of it and sprawling on the floor. I mutter something horribly obscene but it's drowned out by Karen's all-out, hands-to-mouth laughter.

"Did you bang your head?" she asks, catching herself. We help each other up. The fall hasn't harmed me, but my aplomb is shot. I try to save what I can.

"Karen, dearest, we were on the threshold of something profound."

"Tilted at another windmill and missed, huh, my Man of La Mancha?"

If the essence of romance has evaporated, its seeds have been sown. Still, dammit, I missed, well, I missed what I missed.

"It's getting late," Karen says. "April'll be home from school, I have to go." Then she takes my hands in hers and says, "There's hope for us, Ovid Kent." She pulls me down to her, kisses my battered forehead, then turns and starts to walk up the gangplank.

I have the feeling, in this moment, that Karen Knight takes me for being— what's the word I'm looking for?—safe. Safe?

Then she pauses, walks back to me, gives me a very large hug, and whispers, "Thank you, Ovid, for lending an ear." Gently poking her finger into my chest, she adds, "A man never listens better than before he's had sex." She gives me a very serious look that morphs into an adorable grin. Then she turns and completes her exit, mock-sexy again, never looking back.

My eyes follow her all . . . the . . . way . . . down . . . the dock.

When she disappears into the parking lot, I say, out loud, and to no one in particular: "The thresholds come down tomorrow."

That night I sleep the first peaceful sleep I've had in a week.

17.

Karen is more distracting than old Doris has ever been. But, this morning, it's time—past time—to get to work. Notwithstanding, I walk into my library and into further distraction. I'm still in my avoidance mode.

I dust off my O'Hara first editions. I inspect the new, Goodwill-acquired, hundred and fiftieth acquisition to my martini glass collection, nestled in the mahogany case I built long ago and placed between my Nevil Shute and Steinbeck sets. My passion for reading and collecting has supported me reasonably well as a rare book seller, informing my knowledge of the human animal all my life, much as it informed the detecting I did for the DEA. Will it help me now?

The collection, bless it, has nurtured me, too, much as have my books.

Speaking of which, I phone a colleague, Lorne Sterling, at Preston Rare Books in New York to ask if he can do a little better than the eleven thousand he wants for a Whitman-inscribed Leaves of Grass. That's a little out of my league, but I have a buyer for it at twelve, so I can maybe pick up a quick thou.

Lorne can't move on the price. "Send it," I say. "Got anything on Babe Ruth?"

I hear a tap-tap of computer keys. "I can get you a first of "The

Babe Ruth Story." It's inscribed by the Babe himself. Ninety two hundred bucks, but, for . . . "

"Just looking, Lorne. What would Ruth's sig be worth by itself?"

"For you? Three, possibly four thou."

This confirms what I already know. "You sound like you're in business only for me, Lorne. Thanks but no thanks, man. Hey, what if I'd stolen one? Could I dump it on eBay?"

"Are you nuts, Ovid? Smarter to dump it in *the* bay."

"Thanks again, pal. May your stacks soon be empty and your coffers full."

Sell the goods on eBay? Too obvious, of course. Too easy to track. But I can't overlook anything. I pull up Ruth-Cobb-Speaker combo sigs on my Mac. Nothing. I cruise the 'net and send a general inquiry to several dozen of my PADA confreres, professional autograph dealers. Nothing. I hit Bay Area sports memorabilia and trading card shops, coming up empty again. I drop ads on eBay and Craig's List, offering five thou for a Ruth or more for the Babe with other sigs. Don't want to be obvious asking for the trio together, but nothing shows. My hopes are low. If my perp is selling, he's apparently too smart to do it on the net. No more musing. Back to the mansion.

I toss down the last of my Percodans and punch up Milton Blackstone's number. Yes, eleven a.m. would be fine to interview him and John and Thomas or anyone else in the household. Do drop by.

18.

Partly because I'm arriving at Overlook several days late, I arrive twenty minutes early, using the time gained to do a cursory inspection of the estate's perimeter. Stopping at the rear of the grounds I notice, across the broad expanse of lawn, the ladder used to enter John's bedroom window. A towel has been hung over it to keep out the drafts. It's been left in place, apparently for my sake. The walled grounds occupy nearly an acre in a town where lots are boasted of by the square foot. Anyone, determined to do so, could scale walls like these, but I'm certain everything is wired and alarmed throughout. I'll check that out. While this suggests an inside job, I mean to keep an open mind. Video cameras are discreetly placed around the grounds. I'll check with the security people.

After expressing regrets about my accident, Milton Blackstone suggests we take an early lunch. I beg off and ask to be shown the scene of the theft. He lunches, I inspect. Once in John's bedroom, my eye is drawn to the faded spot on the wall where the montage had hung.

I want to memorize the photos of what I saw so I can recognize the montage and sigs if I ever see them again.

"John," I ask, "do you have other pictures of the montage, something more than the two I have?"

He looks mournfully at me. Obviously doesn't like being reminded. Bad start. His mood isn't helping my interrogation. I hear an elevator come to a stop down the hall from his room. A

minute later his father rolls into the room. I'm tempted to inform
him that a morsel of chocolate cake rests in his neat white van
dyke beard, but I let it go. Sensing John's discomfort, the old man
takes the question himself. "I believe there are several pictures,
Mr. Kent. I've had all our valuables photographed. For insurance purposes, naturally." He summons Thomas to fetch the
relevant photos. I'll have them enlarged because I mean to study
them carefully myself.

When I ask him to describe the montage further, he defers
to his son. It's becoming more obvious that Blackstone goes out
of his way to show respect for his son by including him whenever
possible. He's more than a wise man, he is a good father.

John, more at ease now, *always* defers to his father, again
directing his words to him as if Blackstone has never heard them
before. "The montage is twenty four inches wide by thirty six
inches high and has a black frame. It contains four elements.
Two pictures, a pair of Mr. Ruth's ticket stubs to the Cleveland
Indians game at which the oldtimer's game was played, and the
page of autographs. The first element is . . . " He's in a trance now.
He's reciting. ". . . an eight inch by ten inch black and white photo
of Mr. Ruth in uniform standing on the steps of the visitor's
dugout at the old League Park in Cleveland . . . "

I'm looking at the half-sized photo of the montage. It's too
small to make out many details except for the Ruth picture. Ruth
is peering out at something on the field. He's wearing the simple
jersey of his day. Being a road jersey, it lacks the signature
Yankee pinstripes. There were no names on the uniforms in
those days. Unlike now, the team was seen to be more important
than any of its players. The glove he wears looks like one a Little
Leaguer might have received on his ninth birthday. How times
have changed. Gloves today are catching machines. The Bambino has a grim look on his face, as though the Yanks are behind
—something they rarely were back then—and he's determined
to do something about it.

Another photo, smaller, is below and to the left. It's a print of one that a press photographer had taken of Ruth with John at the ballpark that same day. The grinning Bambino is shaking John's hand while engulfing his shoulder with his left arm. I can see that the young John is actually wearing a shy smile. I can't picture John smiling in those days any more than now, but here's the proof.

In the photo's background are several rows of young onlookers, a few of them, girls. Not all are smiling. Some look jealous of the attention the Babe is giving to John. Something tells me that this small photo, though I can barely make out the faces of the people in it, has a certain significance. Another Kent's Rule: Never ignore your hunches.

To the right of this photo are the stubs from the tickets the Babe had given to John that memorable day. John drones on. "At the bottom, in a window that frames the small page of signatures, is the autograph of Mr. Babe Ruth who hit 714 home runs and—"

"Thank you, John," says Blackstone. "That will be sufficient."

I turn back to the spot on the wall. An additional frame hangs next to the empty spot. It holds the scorecard from that day, opened to a spread that also bears the Babe's autograph. It's inscribed "To my pal John Blackstone, Babe Ruth." Why hadn't it been stolen along with the other? Maybe because it didn't fit in the montage? So someone wanted only that montage—maybe only those signatures—very badly.

Are the three sigs on a single sheet more valuable than just the Babe's alone? Usually not, I know this as a dealer, but they apparently are to the someone who risked a great deal to purloin John's proudest possession. The scorecard, because the Babe's inscription is personalized, is likely worth more than the entire contents of the montage, including the three sigs. Hard to figure out why it was left behind. Unless the thief had a very personal reason for wanting only those three autographs; only that more-valuable-than-diamonds set of sigs.

But why?

A long silence follows.

I give up on John for the moment. "Mr. Blackstone, for what amount did the insurance company value the montage?" The old man looks at Thomas. So Thomas is privy to a good deal of financial information regarding his employer's holdings. Worth noting.

"Five thousand dollars," replies Thomas. "For insurance purposes. The insured value—the appraisal—is generally a little higher than the current market value." Thomas knows a lot.

"Was anything else removed from the premises that night?" I ask Blackstone.

"Nothing at all. Odd, now that I think of it. But, if the thief just wanted the autographs, I wonder why he didn't take the scorecard signed by Babe Ruth that hung next to it as well."

I don't reply, but that's exactly what I've been thinking, Mr. B. The signed scorecard, especially with his own name on it, must be at least as important at the montage. Nothing here adds up.

Blackstone goes on. "The montage was there the night before. I know that because I turn off its picture light when I say goodnight to John." I detect a ritual here. "But the next day he was terribly distraught when he came downstairs about ten. He could barely talk." The old man suddenly stops and turns his sad, rheumy eyes to John. Both father and son are tiring now. The elder's mind, clear earlier, is beginning to wander. As is John's. But Blackstone wants to say more.

I wait.

"Finally, that morning, John said to me—over and over —'Babe Ruth . . .'"

John, rocking himself again, breaks in to chant in unison with his father,

". . . is missing . . . Babe Ruth is missing . . . Babe Ruth is missing."

The saddest mantra I've ever heard.

19.

Another long silence. I need help. I try to conjure up the Babe but he must not hear my plea. I'm sure he has his own agenda. "Mr. Blackstone," I say, hoping to discharge the emotion in the air. "Just a few more questions." He nods. "I know your home is wired for protection and has surveillance cameras around the premises. If there was a break-in, why didn't the alarm go off?"

"Thomas will explain," replies Blackstone, tonelessly. He looks at his manservant.

"The alarm did go off, Mr. Kent," says Thomas. It woke me, so I went quickly to turn it off. Of course, I hadn't yet gone to young Mr. Blackstone's rooms. Apparently no one, not even Stinson, was awakened by the alarm. I was going to awaken Mr. Blackstone and await the authorities, but, before I did, I looked out the upper hall window to inspect the grounds and was surprised to see several deer rummaging in the bushes. I found this reassuring."

"Reassuring?"

"Yes. I was certain—well, I assumed—it was they who had set off the alarm. Not wanting to disturb the Blackstones for what I then felt was an unnecessary purpose, I phoned the alarm service to call off their people. They will confirm that. Finally, I reset the alarm and went back to my chambers."

"Without inspecting the premises further?"

"I could hear no noise other than the deer, so I saw no purpose in disturbing others by making a further inspection."

"Do deer or other animals often set off the alarm that way?"

"Well, yes, sir, not often but occasionally. I suppose because of the fences and walls, I've rarely seen any deer on the grounds. But there was an opening, a small breech at the rear of the property where a high, thick hedgerow serves as a wall. Some of the hedgerow plants recently died, and Mr. Mikawa, the gardener, has not yet replaced them. That is where the deer must have entered. And where, I'm afraid, the burglars must have entered."

"Why do you say burglars, Thomas? Things were so quiet, wouldn't it have been more likely there was just one burglar?"

Thomas appears unflustered. "I don't know sir. I suppose you're right."

I make a mental note to question Mikawa about the breech in the hedgerow. "Does the ladder belong to the Blackstones, Thomas?"

"Yes, sir, it does."

Then I ask Blackstone, "Do you take a sedative of any kind?"

"Why, yes I do, Mr. Kent. A mild one, Trazadone. As does John himself, who has trouble sleeping sometimes."

"How do you get this Trazadone?"

"Thomas procures it for me."

"Another question, sir. Have you yet called the authorities? Has a police report been filed?"

I seem to have struck a harsh note. The question brings him back to life. "No, Mr. Kent, I have filed no such report!"

"Why not?" I ask, surprised at the vehemence of his reply. What Blackstone says next makes me feel that, rare lapses aside, this nonagenarian is fully aware of what's going on around him.

"Mr. Kent, in case you're wondering, there was obvious evidence of breaking and entering. The shattered pane in one of John's bedroom windows serves as proof. And there's the ladder, ours though it is. But, had we called the police, I believe they'd

see just an old man and an even older man who had apparently
lost little more than a baseball souvenir. In a nutshell, Mr. Kent,
while the police might have acknowledged the fact of the crime,
I don't believe they'd have taken it seriously, even though it was
perpetrated in such a respectable neighborhood. In my profes-
sion, I've seen this cavalier police attitude all too often. It doesn't
bode well for complainants, nor for the public or for anyone except the police themselves who, though they say they like peace
and quiet, sometimes seem to prefer murder and mayhem to
mere breaking and entering. Uniforms too often generate a
machismo attitude in their wearer, too rarely generating the
responsibility to the public they're supposed to serve, don't you
see?"

I see. At least I think I do. But I hardly agree. I don't see what
he sees. Blackstone's is a rather liberal attitude. I'm something
of a lefty myself, but some of my best friends wear uniforms.

"That's the main reason I called you, not them, Mr. Kent.
There's no reason for you to talk to the police, but you will want
to discuss the contents of the cameras with the surveillance people. Thomas will put you in touch with them."

I was hardly prepared for Blackstone's cynical, even bitter,
tirade. Sea Cliff is hardly the inner city. You'd think the cops in
this 'hood would jump at a thing like this. But experience has
shaped Blackstone's opinions. He obviously doesn't have a warm
relationship with the minions of the law. I'm sure that many of
his clients have been mistreated by same. Anyhow, my fee on my
mind, I'm not inclined to give him an argument.

But, fee or no, I can't help but like this feisty old fellow, this
father who so cherishes his son that he will do—and pay for—
virtually anything to make him whole again.

It's time for the very proper servant. "Thomas, I'd like to talk
with you awhile."

"Certainly, sir, shall I remain here?

"I'd prefer we talk in your own room."

"My chambers, sir?"

Yeah, yeah, your "chambers," Tommy boy. I've caught the man by surprise. Which is the idea.

"They're not too tidy but they're at your disposal, Mr. Kent." John wheels his father away, and I walk Thomas's way.

20.

Not too tidy? Thomas's small suite is immaculate; simply and tastefully decorated, white-glove clean. Is his conscience? Accepting his offer of some sugar-free lemonade, I notice that his refrigerator is as neatly ordered as his rooms. No beer or wine and no liquor visible elsewhere. What are his vices? He might be a tough nut to crack. I take a cursory look around, noticing nothing unusual except a bottle of Trazodone pills next to the lamp on his bed table.

"Thomas?" I say, sipping my lemonade.

"Yes, Mr. Kent."

"Did you steal the autographs?" I shoot from the hip. Kent's Way.

Thomas doesn't flinch. "Good heavens no, sir, I most certainly did not."

"Do you have any idea who may have?" Same wounded reply.

"You weren't there when the theft was discovered by John?"

"No, sir, he was alone, then he came downstairs to tell his father, at which moment I was telling Mr. Blackstone of the alarm, a fact he'll corroborate. We hurried back to Mr. John's room to learn what we could. It was terrible, sir, terrible. I might add that, on the spot, I apologized to Mr. Blackstone for believing that deer had set off the alarm, and for not having gone round to check for a break-in."

"He accepted your apology?"

"He did, sir. He chastised me severely for not waking him, but he seemed to realize there was little we could have done once the thief got away. As you know, he isn't too keen on dealing with the law enforcement people."

Here, Thomas pauses. "Though Mr. Blackstone forgave me, there is something else I must confess."

Confess? Odd word. My eyes narrow.

"It was most foolish of me—Mr. Blackstone's attitude about the law aside— not to at least have summoned the security people immediately. I did, of course, contact them to call them off, but you're the only one who's been called in to investigate this matter."

"I've been out of commission a few days, Thomas. I know the police weren't called the night of the robbery, but you're saying they still don't even know about it?"

The servant appeared surprised at my question. "Why, that's correct, sir, Mr. Blackstone has specifically forbade me to inform them. I certainly would have contacted them had he asked."

Is Thomas being naive or coy? Is he acting? I can't tell. Is there some other reason why Milton Blackstone hates the cops? I don't even want to go there. So I change the subject. "Do you suspect John Blackstone of playing some sort of game here, Thomas?"

"No, sir, I do not," he replies, with some animus in his well-modulated voice. "What would motivate him to do that? I can't imagine Mr. John playing any other than his computer games, something he does incessantly. I do not believe he is capable of devious behavior. He is a gentle and unassuming soul. Though he is growing elderly himself, his mind remains something of a child's. Always will. I'm certain you're aware of that."

Right, Thomas. If I can keep this man talking, maybe he'll reveal something of importance. About himself and, more important, about the theft.

"How long have you been with the Blackstones, Thomas? And, by the way, is Thomas your first or your last name?"

"Twenty-seven years, sir, on the third day of next month. My full name is Cecil Ruggles Thomas."

"You're how old?

"Forty-seven, sir."

"Which means you've spent more than half your life here?"

"I have, indeed, Mr. Kent. I was a young man of nineteen when I arrived from valet school in Bristol, England. The best-paying positions then, as now, were in the United States. Relying upon my school record, Mr. Blackstone hired me before he ever met me, and has been most kind—and generous—to me ever since. My parents are both gone—passed quite early in my life—and he treats me as family, so he and Mr. John are as family to me."

If all this is true, Thomas wouldn't jeopardize such a relationship for the paltry few thou the sigs might bring. Does he stand to inherit from Milton Blackstone? Probably an appropriate sum—generous, likely, based on what Blackstone offered me. Impertinent question to him, but somewhat pertinent to me. So I ask. He tells me he is not privy to that information. Well, we're not talking murder or even natural death here. Nonetheless, this servant is, if a devoted family retainer, hardly part of the Blackstone primogeniture. I doubt if it's a motive worth chasing but I'll put it on the back burner.

What do I have so far? Nothing. Someone wanted the sigs enough to risk prison for them. Why did he want them so badly? That little photo of John and the Babe at the ballpark jumps up in my mind again. But I can't connect it. Does it have something to do with the snatch?

"Is that all, sir?" Thomas stands patiently by while I'm rummaging through my jumbled thoughts.

"Do you have trouble sleeping, Thomas?"

"Why no, sir, I do not."

"But you take sleeping pills every night? I noticed a bottle of Trazodone right next to your bed."

This is the first I've seen Thomas look unsure of himself.

"Well, yes, sir, but not until lately have I experienced a little difficulty falling asleep. My physician recommended them. I took none on the night of the burglary. Is there anything else I can help you with, Mr. Kent?"

"May I see the bottle?" Thomas fetches it. The prescription is made out to him, not to his employer. Lots of pill poppin' at Overlook. Blind alley?

"Thank you, Thomas. As soon as possible I'd like a list of the other people who work in and around the house. Cleaning people, gardeners, like that. And the names of any service people who've visited within the past month, and their contact information. Phone or cable company people, dry cleaners, repairmen, you understand? And of the security company. I'd also like copies of all the phone bills for the past three months including yours and any other employee. Can you try to round all that up for me . . . along with the name and phone number of your prescribing physician?" Doctors don't give out patient information but it doesn't hurt to let Thomas know I'm suspicious of his actions and his motives for them.

"I can indeed, sir. I'll have them for you before you leave. I keep a very careful record of those matters."

"Good, Thomas, I'll be with Mr. Blackstone. One more thing, though. Has anything at the theft site been touched since the theft occurred?"

"No, sir. I've kept Mr. John's room locked when he's not using it. Only Mr. John, Mr. Blackstone, you and I have been in the room since the break-in."

If it was a break-in. So Thomas has a key to John's rooms. Well, why not? Thomas does run the household. "Would you mind bringing me a key to John's rooms, Thomas? I'll wait here till you get it."

The butler nods and leaves. Then I turn the place, but carefully so as to leave it as though it hasn't been searched. Old habit. Part of DEA agent Kent's M.O. On the other hand, would Thomas be more flustered, more vulnerable, if he knew I was searching? Nattering questions like these are part of what drove me into being a bookseller.

I find nothing more suspicious than the pills I've already discovered. It's not unusual for the three of them to be taking a sleeping pill. The key or the small drinking glass I'm about to pocket from his bedstand might carry some of Thomas's liftable prints which I could then compare to those on the window shards. If there are any. I should be so lucky. And what would that really tell me? Am I over-thinking this thing?

Thomas returns with the key.

21.

Approaching John's rooms, I hear a muffled sound. The door is locked. I open it to find the Blackstone scion lying on his bed, folded into himself, moaning, softly and repetitively, "Please come home, Mr. Ruth, please come home . . ." Stinson lies next to him, whimpering in sympathy.

Should I leave him alone? I can't. "I'm sorry to disturb you, John, but I need to look around. Is that OK with you?"

For an answer, John mumbles through a towel he's pressing to his mouth, "It's him, I know it's him. I know who it is. You have to get him."

"Him, John? Who is 'him'"

But, instead of an answer. His next words are, shrieked, "I want to die, I want to die!" When I rush to console him, I see that the towel he's holding to his wrist is slightly bloody. I snatch the towel away and roll him onto his back. A pair of children's scissor lies next to him.. The points are rounded and incapable of inflicting any real damage. But, using the scissors, obviously, he's managed to open a shallow wound on his left wrist.

I immediately call in Blackstone and Thomas. The father almost faints at the sight of his son's blood. Thomas, after attending to the wound and helping John to bed, leaves the room. I wheel Blackstone into John's anteroom to discuss this latest crisis. He looks older even than his ninety-one years. Totally defeated.

"Mr. Blackstone, I'm terribly sorry this has happened, but I must ask, has anything like it ever happened before?"

"Before the theft?" replies the distraught Blackstone. "No, no, never, not in all his years on earth. But, late last night, he woke me with his crying. He's not a good sleeper. He said then, as he keeps saying now, that he wants to die. I didn't take him seriously, though I most certainly should have. What do you propose I do, Mr. Kent?" The words are a desperate plea, not a question.

"He just told me he knows who did it. Have you any idea what he's talking about?"

"No, none whatsoever. But I don't want you to keep asking him, it will only upset him more. Frankly, I doubt if he does know. He lives mostly in his mind."

I am no longer looking at "Blackstone the Logician," just at a despondent old man at life's—and wit's—end. "Mr. Blackstone, I strongly urge you to put John into a specialist's hands. Your son is grieving over the autographs as surely as he would over the loss of real people he loves. His Asperger's may be partly responsible for what seems to be an over-reaction, but his symptoms must be dealt with. It's obvious that John is dangerous to himself. If those had been real scissors he might have killed himself."

Blackstone, looking ashamed of his own inaction, agrees with my lay analysis. "I fully understand, Mr. Kent. However feeble John's suicide attempt is, it is a cry for help that I must clearly heed." He then accepts my offer to call in Edward Diavalone, my neuropsychologist friend whom I'll soon be hitting up in search of behavioral clues. To the thief's behavior, not John's.

I ring up Eddie, sweet-talk his receptionist into putting the busy man on, quick-feed him the background, then turn the phone over to my client so an appointment for John can be arranged.

When Blackstone leaves, I use my old fingerprint kit, first to do a thorough dusting of the wall where the framed montage had hung. John's hooded eyes follow me, but only halfheartedly. What the hell did he really mean by "I know who it is?" Does he really? And now Blackstone doesn't want me to pump him. Then suddenly, John says, in his peculiar flat voice, but through clenched teeth, "It was the boy I gave the tickets to. It was him. I know it."

I humor him. "You sound like you saw him do it, John. Did you?"

Not looking at me, not hearing me, he repeats, "It was the boy I gave the tickets to."

Can I tell him how impossible that would be? Instead, I ask, "Do you know his name?"

Now he does turn to me. His widened eyes tell me I'm crazy for asking, "How would I know that?" he says. Then, before burying his head in his pillow, he tells me to go away.

❏

Before I leave the room I gather the few shards of glass left on the sill of the broken, single-paned lower window and place them in a plastic box, afterward dusting the unbroken upper pane and its surround. The perp might have entered and exited the room through this window, but he could have entered through one of the others which might have been unlocked. I dust those, too, though they're all securely locked. Still, someone could have come in anywhere, even through the front door. With a little help from a friend.

I lean out the broken window to see what lies below. Even from this height, I can see some glass on the ground below the window. I'll check and dust it later.

Thomas returns with the list of names I'd requested.

"Thomas," I ask, "is John a good sleeper?"

"Usually, yes. He often sleeps ten hours a night without waking. That is normal, I believe, for one with his condition." That's funny. John's father says he's not a good sleeper. Curiouser and curiouser this becomes.

"Does Stinson sleep with him?"

"Yes, sir, always. Sometimes on the bed, sometimes on the floor next to the bed."

"Doesn't he bark or something in the presence of strangers?"

Thomas shrugs. "He rarely barks and he's not often in the presence of strangers."

"What hour does John usually go to bed?"

"Generally at nine or ten, sir."

"But that means he slept twelve, thirteen hours the night of the break-in. Doesn't that strike you as being beyond the usual?"

"Not necessarily, Mr. Kent. He often plays that electronic baseball of his for hours after retiring. It consumes him, but apparently helps bring on sleep. I wasn't in his rooms to know when he actually dropped off. It might even have been past midnight."

"And the break-in occurred at . . . ?"

"Three-twenty a.m. The security people said their records showed that as the time the alarm went off."

"Thank you, Thomas. That will be all. For now."

❏

I spend the rest of the day questioning the other members of the household. Marcella Blanek is the head housekeeper, the only other full-timer who lives at Overlook. She's a tall, blocky woman of nondescript age. She's been with the Blackstones for over ten years. The night of the theft was prior to her day off. She'd left early that evening to visit her sister Olga at a Jehovah's Witnesses gathering in Petaluma where she'd stayed the entire next day, arriving home long after the theft had occurred. I ask for Olga's particulars as well as Marcella's. Marcella could have made a clandestine return in the wee hours. But her alibi is later substantiated by her sister.

22.

Next morning, I meet with Charles Mikawa, the gardener. Mikawa is an experienced and sophisticated craftsman. Beyond his twenty weekly hours at the mansion, he finds time to operate a small home woodshop, using his extensive knowledge of Japanese joinery to create exquisite outdoor furniture, mainly teak tables and Torii arches. He does not live on the premises and was in his shop alone during the evening in question. He says his wife and children were also home and will vouch for his being there. I don't waste time contacting them. The gardener seems legit.

Mikawa has two part-time helpers, Guatemalans, whose names and numbers he gives me. He shows me the breech in the rear hedgerow, and admits that deer—which were rarely a problem before the unusual death of his shrubbery— had been sneaking in lately at night to feast on his flowers. He claims he hasn't been remiss in repairing the breech, he's simply waiting for the new hedges to be delivered.

This isn't, according to Mikawa, the first time wild animals have set off the Blackstone alarms. This checks with what Thomas has told me. They have a way of getting in that mystifies even him. The mansion borders on the thickly wooded Presidio, rife with deer, with all kinds of wildlife. If they can get in undetected, so can a man. Or men.

"May I go, Mr. Kent? I have much work to do."

"Thank you, Mr. Mikawa."

❏

According to Thomas, during the weeks prior to the theft, several service people had visited Overlook, some more than once: the grocer's delivery man, the UPS guy and a pizza truck to deliver the one dish that—I come to learn through a quick phone call— John Blackstone cannot live without: pizza with sausage, pepperoncini and black olives. Thank you for the fascinating details, pizza man. These people have neither the occasion nor the right to visit the second floor of the mansion. Except for John's Babe Ruth story being on the radio once, and in a book, none of them would likely have known about the autographs, and certainly not of their whereabouts in the mansion. I'd get to them all for questioning—maybe—but I hold little hope of learning anything worthwhile.

My trip to Bell Security, whose state-of-the-art hi-tech alarm systems protect half of Sea Cliff's wealthy residents, makes me waste a few hours reviewing their tapes for the hours immediately before and after the theft. They reveal nothing, no human activity, and no animal activity either, as in deer. Carl Bell, the company's owner, explains that there are only half a dozen cameras around the Blackstone grounds, mostly at the gate, the front and the other entrances: none directed specifically at John's bedroom windows. It's simply impractical to train a camera on every window. Thus the gap in coverage. But, maybe because the tapes reveal nothing, they reveal a lot.

❏

There had been two personal visitors, Conrad and Laura Cunningham, a couple in their sixties, who had been to dinner two weeks earlier. Laura Parsons Cunningham is the daughter of the late Mrs. Blackstone's closest friend since childhood, Jocelyn Parsons, who died some years earlier. The Cunninghams live several doors down in the family home inherited by Laura who, as a child, played there with her slightly older friend, John Blackstone. Before Mrs. Blackstone died so tragically, Laura swore to her that she and her mother, Jocelyn, would always look in on John and Mr. Blackstone. To this day, the Cunninghams and the Messrs. Blackstone often exchange dinner visits. These details are included in the meticulous notes the accommodating Thomas has presented me.

I'll arrange to meet with Laura Cunningham and look forward to her personal insights on her neighbors, my clients.

Before leaving, I do another perimeter search, spiraling in to the ladder leaning against the wall. I seems to mock me, a reminder of the critical signatures I'm no closer to retrieving.

I look behind the bushes under the ladder and find the broken shards I'd seen from John's window. Handling them by their edges I place them in a red rope envelope and leave to do some homework.

23.

Next day, I wake up early. On my mind is Karen. A picnic. Limantour Beach, maybe. A nice chilled Vouvray, an aged chevrot, a baguette, a long walk hand-in-hand on the sand, some . . . But I've got to remain focused. I'll call her later. Right now I need Leo.

Leo Cavanaugh and I have been pals since the old neighborhood in North Beach in the city. Played a lot of softball and basketball together. We both wanted to be cops. He became one, I went with the DEA. He got me information only available on the street and the quid pro his quo was, I did favors for Leo that an Oakland lieutenant of detectives is not allowed to do for himself. Such as using my hands to extract information from reluctant snitches. Such as . . . but that, too, is for another telling.

I call him.

"Leo, you over-the-hill flatfoot, when are you going to sell out and get a respectable six-figure job in private industry like your smarter blues?"

"When pigs fly," says Leo, laconically. He never reaches far for a metaphor. Been using that one for the thirty years we've known and loved each other. "What can I do to you, sweetheart?"

"So glad you asked, darling. I need rundowns on a bunch of people. Looking for an autograph thief."

"Someone swiped your wares?" Leo says.

"Not mine, my client's. Milton Blackstone. Know him?"

"Know him?" whistles Leo. "He ruined enough of my convictions to hold back my sergeant stripes for years. He had to retire before I could make it to looie. Toughest old bird I ever dealt with, but fair, always fair. Give me what you got and I'll get back to you. In fact," he says, "come by the house tonight and you can have the answers *and* mom's Irish stew. Fresh soda biscuits, that special gravy, the works."

I recall that Karen is working tonight. "Name your time, Lieutenant. And don't be surprised if, under the influence of my favorite meal, I run off with my favorite cook."

"If mom could run, she'd be the first to suggest it. I don't know what she sees in your sorry ass, pally, but every time you come by you seem to take twenty years off the eighty-three she's piled on. You got a certain appeal for old broads, Ov. Only reason I invite you is that I know the stew will come out even better if you're there. Be over by six."

"How's Mary Ann? I may run off with her instead." I'm kidding on the square. Fact is, I've always been a little in love with Leo's gorgeous wife, Mary Ann. Saint Mary, he calls her—we all do—for putting up with the likes of him. And even more for being able to live with his mother, Bridget.

Bridie, as Mother Cavanaugh prefers to be known, is a real piece of work. Talk about your feisty, I sometimes wonder if Bridie actually *is* coming on to me. But, damn, the woman can cook. Irish stew? Child's play. The old gal can whip up a Mexican pozole blindfolded or a pan-fried monkfish that would earn her sous chef status at Chez Panisse.

I give my input of names and the dope I'm looking for to Leo, issue a final, highly personal insult, then hang up.

What next? Get back to Ed Diavalone to profile my perp. Then back to the Internet to check on the E-trades and webs. A waste likely. But necessary.

No picnic this afternoon. I call Karen and let her know. She understands, or says she does.

❏

This evening, promptly at six, my hair combed almost flat, I stand at Leo's door with a bottle of *nigori-zake*—cloudy sake—in hand. A quirky hostess gift, but a favorite of the even quirkier Bridie Cavanaugh. Mary Ann lets me in. She's been married to Leo for over twenty years, but looks twenty years younger. They never had kids. She says he's all the kid she needs. An aerobics instructor since before she met him, she has a strong body and an even stronger mouth, not unlike Bridie's, but it's the only thing she and Bridie have in common.

She offers her sympathies about my busted head, then adds: "But when the hell are you going to join my exercise club? You ever notice how 'ab' is hiding in the word 'flab?'"

"Are you trying to tell me something, my dear Mary Ann? 'Ab' is also found in 'fabulous' which, as you know, I am. Say, is that a white hair I spy among your golden strands?"

"C'mon, Ovid, can the malarkey and don't change the subject. Come say hi to Leo. Maybe we can make passes at each other while he watches the Knicks destroy his real beloveds, the Warriors. He'll never notice."

Sometimes, when she talks like that, I'm not sure if Saint Mary's kidding. "I don't mess with married chicks," I say, "unless they mess with me first. Now, where's the *real* love of my life?"

"Bridie's in the kitchen stirring the sauce as usual. Enter at your own risk."

I steal up behind Bridie and swipe the wooden spoon she's using to stir the oniony sauce of her stew, tasting it before she can react. Then I whisper into her ear, "I'll love you forever, Bridie Cavanaugh . . . if you'll just add a pinch of sriracha. Have you micks never heard of spice?"

For my good advice, she snatches her spoon back and feints a poke at my privates. "That," she informs her assailant, in a brogue that sounds filtered through a peat bog, "is how I handled the laddies in Limerick when they snuck up on me as you just did. Now, can you act normal and say hello with just a simple kiss on the cheek? I do accept ear nibbles."

"Just for that, Bridie, I'm going to drink half your sake." She screams with feigned delight when I pull the bottle from behind my back, snatching it out of my hand and cradling it like it was in infant in swaddling clothes. "We can take it back to my place later," I add, "after we put your kids to bed."

"Don't try to con me, Kent? All you're takin home is left-overs . . . if you leave any." She and my neighbor, Ethel, are sort of bookends. "Now get yourself to the family room and swap your usual insults with my couch potato son. I'll feed you when I'm good and ready. Shoo!"

Bridie may be 83, but she's not old. She recently told me she still uses a vibrator.

❑

Leo is flipping the TV set off when I walk in. "Ain't nobody can beat my Warriors!"

"My Cavs will beat 'em in the finals." You can't take the boy out of Cleveland. "But greetings to you, too, Leo." I slam together a quick martini. "You oughta keep your gin in the freezer, lieu-tenant of detectives. The frost lets you see whose fingerprints are on the bottle."

"Yours are the only prints ever been there, Ov. Who else drinks that swill? When are you going to start drinking beer like a real man, instead of those sissy cock-tails?"

"Beer makes me fart, Leo. I notice it does the same to you. Now, can we talk about what you dug up for me today, or must I keep pretending I actually enjoy your conversation?"

"Here's what I got for you, pally." Leo is still a devotee of Sinatra. "Regarding the service people who showed during the month prior, they're all clean. Couple of MVs, that's it. No felonies. Blanek the housekeeper is OK but her sister Olga once spent a night in the slammer for beating up her neighbor. Mikawa, the gardener, his helpers, none have a record. One of the helpers is an illegal but that ain't my department. If they have friends, cousins, whatever, you'll have to supply more names. By the way, you said you were checking the phone bills so I didn't bother. Did any strange out-of-town numbers turn up?

"Don't know," I say. "Only had time to glance at them. It's amazing how little the Blackstones use the phone. I'll leave the bills for you to re-check. So what about Thomas? Cecil Thomas?"

Leo turns to me, blinking. "You're looking at me like you think the butler did it. C'mon, Ov." A small grin breaks through the serious look on his face. "Did a thorough check on him. Found out where he spends his time off. Cecil Thomas appears to be what he appears to be. His story checks out and he's never had so much as a jaywalking ticket. From everything you've told me, and from what I've found, he sounds too good to be true. Also, I checked out his bank accounts. No large recent deposits. By the way, judging by the bar where he hangs out—*when* he hangs out anywhere—he's probably gay."

"Yeah, my gaydar gets that, but it doesn't suggest anything. I didn't even think he drank. Gay's a slippery slope, Leo, y'know? Especially in this town. Does that 'too good to be true' persona look fishy to you in any other way."

"Everything looks fishy to me. But couldn't the perp be just some second story bum who made a random hit for a few bucks? The obvious isn't always the wrong way to go. Occam's . . ."

". . . Razor," I finish. Leo and I think alike, always have. "Not likely, friend. The thief left behind another Babe Ruth sig worth more than the one stolen. Anyhow, if it *was* a random theft, it doesn't leave me with any real clue, any telling motive. Was he in it for the money? Did he want the autographs for another reason? The answers should be obvious, but they're not."

Mary Ann walks in with some peeled shrimp. The shop-talk stops. I've got all I can from Leo.

Maybe it's the second helping of stew or the peach cobbler.

More likely, the second martini. I feel a bulge in my belly, a blip in my already rattled brain, and the need to excuse myself early.

A handshake from Leo, a hug from Mary Ann, a slap on my backside from Bridie, and I'm out of there.

❏

I'm digging for the Alka at eleven p.m. Bad as I feel, I polish off last Sunday's New York Times acrostic. Acrostics keep my mind sharp. At least this is what I keep telling myself.

But I can't get my mind off my unsolved Babe Ruth puzzle.

24.

"The lunch is on me, Eddie."

I'm sitting with Edward Diavalone the next day studying the chalkboard at Teyaki. Teyaki may be the smallest sushi shop in San Francisco, but it's the best, guaranteed. And the least known. It doesn't even post its name out front. No menu either.

We're sitting at one of the only three tables in the joint. Eddie's stolen an hour to let me pick his brains. He seems delighted with this respite from his grinding neuropsychology practice.

"Doesn't need a menu, Edward, it's mostly omakase. Teyaki is Japanese for 'homemade.' Nomi serves what he chooses." A plate of seared uni is set in front of us. The sex glands of the sea urchin, the foie gras of the sea. Then his wife, Aiko, brings us a magnificent crisped sea bass plated to look like it's rising from the ocean. Reminds me, with a shiver, of old Doris.

I get down to business, first filling Eddie in on the situation. "You'd know how the kind of guy I'm looking for thinks. What kind of a low-life would risk hard time to steal a thing like a cherished set of autographs? Can you profile him for me?"

"Well, the obvious reason to steal is for gain, Ovid. But it could be for other reasons, personal ones. For attention, revenge or jealousy."

"If this were for gain," I say, "the perp would be relatively easy to find, especially if he tries to sell on the open market. But I've checked the E-markets, the whole damned Internet, and sent an E-trace out to virtually every baseball memorabilia shop in the country. Canvassed my sig dealer pals, too and come up empty. What were the other reasons to steal; attention, revenge, jealousy?"

"Yeah, if any of those are the motive, you have a problem."

"This I already know, Edward."

"A small problem, Ov. Not to worry. If the purpose is attention or recognition, he'll show himself sooner or later. If you're lucky, he's in that category. If it's revenge or jealousy, that wouldn't make him too hard to discover either. He'd want to reveal the theft so he could flaunt it to make his victim feel its loss. Faith, my boy."

Eddie hesitates, looks at the ceiling then snaps his fingers. "Wait a minute, there could be another reason. If his purpose is that he covets autographs just to have them, to look at them and touch them just like John Blackstone does, then he'd keep the theft quiet for fear of their being taken away from him. If that's why he did it, you really will have trouble finding him."

"But, Edward, anyone would covet a Babe Ruth autograph, maybe just because it's worth a lot of bucks. Still, you don't go breaking into a home to steal it."

"Not so, Ovid. Some people—not just your typical thief— would do exactly that if the object meant enough to them. To someone like that, the desire for *pos*session becomes *ob*session. He might steal it even if he'd never done such a thing before."

"The guy's obsessive? The thought that he might want the sigs for himself has actually occurred to me."

"Could be. And he's probably compulsive, too. They go together, you know. It might have driven him crazy that he hadn't completed some kind of a Hall-Of-Fame set of autographs. Or had a chance to obtain the stolen object before his victim obtained it."

"So about this possibly obsessive-compulsive thief, how does his mind work?"

"Sorry, Ov, that's the part I'm never sure about. People in my field have been trying to figure out how the criminal mind works for centuries. We know what criminals do, the M.O., but we don't know everything about the *why*. Maybe the thief is just a base-ball nut like your John. Could even be that similar autographs had been stolen from or lost by the thief and he wants to replace them, or that the real ones belonged to the thief in the first place." Eddie hesitates. Or . . ."

"Or?"

"Or I simply don't know."

"But you're not suggesting that John Blackstone stole the autographs from the thief to begin with, are you? John didn't steal *or* buy them, he got them himself from the old time players themselves, this I do happen to know. What *are* you suggesting, Eddie, that the thief *thinks* John stole the autographs from him?"

"Maybe."

"Why would he think that when it isn't true?"

"Because," says Eddie, tapping his temple, "he might have become delusional, a point I haven't yet made. Because some-times you want something so much you can taste it, so you begin to think you deserve it, it *should* be yours, that it's *meant*—by some divine provenance—to be yours. Finally you believe it *is* yours. The wish becomes the reality. Belief transference. 'I wish it was mine' becomes 'it *is* mine!' capeesh? That's the nature of delusion, especially of obsessive delusion."

"I think I understand," I say. "If this obsessed person has convinced himself that the autographs are his own, he feels he's got the right to have them back, even to steal them back. In his mind he's not stealing anything, he's only retrieving what already belongs to him. Which, to him, is no crime at all."

"That's it precisely, my friend. That's the transference part. Later it can become an actual transference of the desired object; a *theft*. And if the guy truly believes he should own the object, he could go even farther to retrieve it. If he were seriously demented as well as deluded, the crime of retrieval could be worse than mere theft, it could result in mayhem or murder, whatever it takes to get the thing back. Depends on his state of mind."

"Swell. So how do I find the guy?"

"You mean that rhetorically, don't you? I don't know, Ovid, you're the one playing detective, you figure it out. Just remember, these are just theories. Maybe the servant did do it. Maybe you oughtta stick to rare books."

"That's cruel, Edward." Then I tell him about John's insistence that the thief was the boy he gave his old-timers game tickets to.

"Someone like John doesn't lie, Ov. He may see that boy in his mind's eye, but he does see him. And intuits that he wanted John's autographs badly enough to steal them. The fifty-year time difference may mean nothing to John, because, at times, he seems to be living back then."

"So a guy comes out of a fifty-year past to steal John's sigs."

"Could be. In John's mind. Listen, my friend, thanks for the superb lunch, I gotta go, my couch runneth over."

I call for the check. Aoki drops it off along with the requisite fortune cookies. "I thought you said this place was Japanese," says Eddie. "What's with the fortune cookies?"

"This place is anything Nomi says it is."

I open my cookie and read it to Eddie. "A friend will be helpless in solving a baffling problem," I lie.

Eddie harrumphs. "Mine says I'm going to meet a beautiful woman. Really."

No sooner said than Nomi's daughter, Tamiko, a graduate student at Berkeley, bursts through the rear door. She grabs an apron, then, at her father's whispered directions, comes immediately to collect my waiting cash. No plastic here. "Hi, Mr. Kent, we've missed you."

"Hi, Tammy, how's your doctoral thesis going?"

"Quite well. But I'm tripping over the Abnormal Psych."

"Well, coincidence of coincidences, here's the man who can help you. This is my abnormal friend, Edward Diavalone. A neuropsychologist."

Eddie offers a shy hello to Tamiko. He's never been very good with women. Such is the way sometimes with shrinks. Seems he can only figure them out if he sees them by appointment. To make him even more nervous in the presence of this woman, she's drop-dead gorgeous. He needs to bolt but he's reluctant to leave.

He says he finds Teyaki's food quite good. He tells me he'll try it again, maybe. Tomorrow, maybe.

25.

I shove Eddie's troubling revenge/jealousy theory aside, prefer-
ring his obsessive/compulsive take. Neither are much to go on.
No luck with the Internet, either, but the basic theft-for-cash
slant is a rock I have to keep lifting.

Since I'm already in the city, I'll hit a few trading card shops.
I still have to acknowledge the possibility that the thief is local,
unsophisticated and dumb enough to sell locally. "The obvious
isn't always the wrong way to go." That's what Leo had said.
Finding the shops is easy. Finding parking in this sardined city
is something else. Eight hundred thousand cars, six hundred
thousand slots to fit 'em.

Norm's Kards, Komics & Kollectibles on 24th in SOMA
seems a likely starting place. Or not. It's badly lit and so packed
with dusty cartons of sports cards and ancient comics I can hardly find a place to stand. I flash my old DEA license and ask the
tall, skinny kid behind the counter if I can see the proprietor.
"You're lookin' at him," he says, without looking up from an old
Harvey Pekar "American Splendor." The kid might be twenty.

"You Norm?"

"Nope."

"What happened to Norm?" I ask, not giving a damn.

"Sold out to a guy named Al. Who sold out to me." This I don't
plan to pursue. "I'm Freddie. You buyin' or sellin'," he says, not

giving a damn. The kid looks like he's suffering from early onset osteoporosis. "Or are you here just to ask questions?"

I'm here to make silly putty out of your pimply face. "I'm here to ask questions, son. You OK with that?"

"Depends," says Freddie, examining his nonexistent fingernails for a good spot to continue nibbling.

I pull out the photograph. "Ever see anything like this sheet of autographs?"

"Nope," Freddie says, hardly looking. Finally, he squints at it through his close-set eyes. "Never heard of Speaker. Never seen him on a card." This guy trades baseball cards? I'm wondering if he's ever heard of the Babe.

Then, for no discernible reason, Feckless Freddie opens up. "Shops like mine don't do much with sigs, y'know? Our signed bats, balls, jerseys, like that—even our cards—come mostly from jobbers, guys who get 'em in lots and wholesale 'em to dealers like me. But I mostly deal in, like, hip comics, old movie posters, like that."

"Well, if I were to offer you the original of this sheet of autographs, what might it be, like, worth?"

Freddie eyeballs it again. "What you got here is an oddy, a group of sigs. Worth less than the total of the singles. And sigs are worth more if they're personalized. Like 'to Freddie from his pal, Barry Bonds.'

"But the price for these?"

"Three, maybe four thou. Separately, maybe two-and-a-half, three apiece, except for the . . ."

"Tris Speaker."

"Yeah. Now, your rookie Ruth card, when he broke in with the Red Sox, it's worth a whole lot more. And if you was to bring me a Honus Wagner we could be talkin' a hundred thou. Only a few around. You ever hear of Wagner?"

This putz obviously isn't aware that the last Hans Wagner rookie card recently went for three mill, as in million, the most by far for any sports card in history. Wouldn't mind having brokered that one myself. "I thank you for your invaluable input, Freddie. May a Honus be your bonus and a Batman Number One come floating through your transom."

"What's a transom?" I hear as I walk out the door.

I hit a few more places. No luck. Then I cross the bridge, collect an In-N-Out cheeseburg, fries and shake for an early dinner, then home to fret about still standing on square one. Which inspires the building of a Kentish martini of colossal proportions.

But, per Kent's Law, only one.

26.

Next morning, after breakfasting on Pepto-Bismol and some unidentified remains from the fridge, I phone the Cunninghams, the old friends of the Blackstones. Yes, they'd been there after the theft, had been fully informed of it and of course would fully cooperate with my investigation. And, yes, they'd be delighted to meet with me at eleven this very morning.

The Cunningham's are next door, a few acres down from the Blackstones. I'm allowed in by a downstairs maid or housekeeper—I'm still trying to keep these job descriptions straight—and am led into the den to be greeted by Laura Cunningham, wearing black tights and a long silk blouse. Her husband, Conrad, bent over at his desk, is at least ten years older than the early sixties she looks to be. He welcomes me offhandedly, not getting up. His face is buried in a laptop whose screen is filled with stock graphs. He soon excuses himself to "work in my study."

The thought comes to me that these people must have rooms where they go just to scratch their ass.

"Now, Mr. Kent," says Laura Cunningham, "what can I tell you that will possibly help you regain what John Blackstone has lost?"

"First, thanks for seeing me, Mrs. Cunningham."

"I'll call you Ovid if you'll call me Laura," she replies, settling herself into a huge stuffed chair and tucking her shapely legs beneath her. "I will do anything to help my John." She's a handsome and well-composed woman, tall, slim and patrician-looking, nicely maintaining an attractive, youthful face and figure in spite of her years. God-made or store-bought? I imagine her perfectly at ease hosting a party for a hundred Sea Cliff intimates. I also see that this woman can still attract men as moths to light.

Knowing how close Laura Cunningham is to the Blackstones, I have no qualms about revealing the details of my investigation to her. Milton Blackstone has, in fact, urged me to do so. I update her fully. Her reply is to sit pensively, listen, then offer me coffee and scones.

A loaded tray is summoned from the kitchen. Laura says, "I made these myself, you know." I do my best to visualize her baking them, but the picture won't focus. Remembering my anti-breakfast, I gingerly pluck a few scones off the tray and thank her, then try to bite into them. "Very tasty," say I.

After we settle in, Laura looks straight at me. "Ovid Kent," she says, "I doubt there's a thing I can say to move your investigation forward. I noticed nothing unusual in the neighborhood on the night of the theft. But there is something I must tell you."

"I'm listening, Laura." What does a woman mean when she addresses you by your full name that way?

"Other than his father, no one has been closer to John Blackstone throughout his life than me. He's older but I've always thought of him as a little brother. We grew up together—even if his condition hasn't quite allowed him to grow up. I love John Blackstone. I believe I know how his mind works. For you and I to have suffered the loss of these autographs, however precious we may have held them, would be to have suffered not much more than the loss of a thing, an object. If one of my Han Dynasty urns were to be stolen or broken, I'd be upset, yet I'd get over it. And besides, objects are insured, as John's autographs must be."

She says "ob-jays" for objects. Isn't the way I'd say it.

"But, to John," she continues, "those autographs are hardly a 'thing.' They're the center of his life, as his mother had once been so very long ago. He treats them as people do a religious triptych, an icon, an object of worship." This time she says object right.

There was that reference to obsession that Eddie Diavalone had brought up. It didn't take a shrink to figure out the meaning of the montage to John Blackstone. Laura Cunningham is obviously attuned in to it, and totally groks John himself.

She goes on. "I believe it's fair to say that John has doted upon the signatures as one would upon a spouse, a parent, a child. In the convoluted labyrinth of his mind, he has treated the autographs as though they were a kidnapped child. Do you follow me, Ovid. Do I sound like an armchair psychologist?"

I follow her. "I follow you, Laura. I'd reached the same conclusion. Fact is, though it could be beside the point, John Blackstone may not be the only one who's obsessed over the montage. Whoever stole it may have been obsessing over it almost as much as John. But what's the upshot? What do *you* conclude?"

"Just this . . ." Laura hesitates before going on. "Losing a child can drive any parent to madness. Or worse. For John to have lost this particular 'child' has caused him a degree of grief that may drive him over the edge. What I'm saying is that the loss can literally kill him. Ovid, I believe he's capable of making another suicide attempt, less feeble than the first. Yes, Milton told me about that. I've seen John since the theft and I've never seen him so down, so despondent. I know what I'm talking about. I have no proof of my contention, it's just my intuition. But I feel it strongly."

Her next words, if spoken softly, are firm. She leans forward and looks right at my eyes. "You, sir, must find these autographs that are so important to John. How much clearer can I make it? I'm sorry to burden you with my contention, but I do believe that John's life—his very life—depends upon your retrieving what he's lost."

I'm moved by her last remark. "I hear you, Laura." I truly wish I hadn't. My hand goes to loosen the collar I'm not wearing.

"If you'd like, and if it's all right with Mr. Blackstone, I'll keep you and your husband informed."

"Don't bother with Connie, just keep in touch with me." Her tone dismisses him as if he too is a servant. Then she arises, the hostess in perfect control, to indicate that the visit is over. "Thank you, Ovid, I hope I've been able to offer something of value. Here, I'm wrapping the rest of these scones for you to take home."

I leave with a feeling less of purpose than of hopelessness. I've learned something important about John Blackstone, but what I've learned is very troubling. The pressure to do what I've contracted to do, and do it quickly, is building. And now I have a thief who may kill his victim by retaining the autographs, and a victim who may kill him*self* if they're not returned. And who am I kidding, I have no thief. So keep thinking, Mr. Autograph Sleuth, keep thinking.

Still, the only new thought that comes to me as I drive home is that the scones tasted like my second grade paste pot. I know what can wash that taste out. Too bad it's seven hours till drinkie time.

❏

Back home, after portsiding the pastry, I study the photos awhile. The Babe's signature had been written with a slightly shaky hand. Then I recall that he was ill when he signed it. Does this factor into anything? Babe, if you can hear me, come on down.

My mind goes back to the evidence I found at the Blackstone residence. Broken glass on the ground, broken glass on the sill, prints. With that and the possible motives suggested by Ed Diavalone I still have very little. Part of me wants to run, to pretend I'd never gotten involved. But I'm now deeply and personally involved. With the Blackstones, even the disdainful Stinson, and now I have someone new to disappoint, Laura Cunningham.

And, of course, if I need something else to think about, there's a different kind of loss than the sigs: the serious reduction of a big, fat, beautiful fee.

27.

For the next two days, I continue to spin my wheels. I chase down more card and autograph dealers, more to keep moving than to uncover leads. I re-question the Overlook staff and service people, all to no avail. An UPS driver had been called by Thomas for a pickup shortly after the theft. Had the montage been hidden in the home and expressed somewhere? Turns out Thomas had returned some video baseball games that hadn't sat too well with John.

Thinking that this perp, if as obsessed as I think he could be, might be capable of serious violence if personally confronted, I decide to check out a piece, a handgun. I was never very good with one I had at the DEA, an old military .45. I drop into Straight Shooter, a combination gun shop and indoor shooting range up in San Rafael. The owner, Ray Simovic, after citing a litany of gun safety rules, fixes me up with a Ruger automatic that sits pretty well in my hand. We move out to the range. He fits me with ear plugs, racks up an Alco Rapid-Fire paper target with a bad-guy silhouette in black on an orange background, sends it fifty feet down-range, shows me how to hold the piece with two hands, movie style, to steady it, then nods for me to commence rapid fire. I aim and pull the trigger eight times in quick succession. The kick alone suggests I haven't done too well.

The target comes back without a single hole in its head or its

heart, but its entire scrotum has been smithereened. I'm beginning to think this is a very bad idea. I pass on the piece, buy a
Straight Shooter bullet on a beaded keychain to remind myself
never again to carry, then pay Simovic for his trouble. His head
is wagging as I head out the door.

Normally, I'm very disciplined when it comes to my professional work. It never bothered me to do sixteen-hour days when
I was tracking a drug dealer. Or, later, tracking down a set of
first editions for a deep-pocketed client.

But, as much as I need discipline now, I can't get Karen out
of my head. Though I try to set aside her unforgettable face, it
keeps appearing on my inner screen. Why, I ask myself? Karen
Knight is about as solidly fixed in my life as Babe Ruth. Slight
difference; my arms have never been full of the Babe.

Is this, I'm thinking, about love, or maybe just about *making*
love? Is it another Kent infatuation? Am I in love with love
again? Well, how would I know? Is Karen real? Is the Babe? What
the hell *is* real? This crazy quest is real, that's what's real! That
was some bump I got on my head.

The dilemma suggests I pour my Gordon's earlier than the
usual big-hand-up-small-hand-down. The sun may not yet be
below the yardarm but, with my recliner embracing me, and my
fingers on my Partega cigar, my troubles begin to rise like a
Babe-blown smoke ring.

Then that face I've memorized, reappears. Dammit, I have
to be with her. Now. I have to tell her how I feel. She's coming off
nights tomorrow. And hasn't she mentioned something about a
few weeks coming to her soon? I have got to call her now.

But my second martini insists I keep reclining. I wake up at
1 a.m., too late to call, she's working. I mutter an unflattering
description of myself, grab a salami on rye and the dregs of some
cole slaw from last week's KFC binge, then drag myself off to bed,
practically breaking my right toe on my Great Wall of China.

Bad words follow.

❏

A dreamless night clears up nothing. My head is splitting, but it's no longer the concussion. I do my best to gather my scattered wits. I call Karen.

"Good morning, my dear," I purr into my cell. "Miss you. Can't think, sleeping about you." Beautiful. Lounge lizard strikes again. Idiot, gather your wits!

"Very funny. But I've been thinking about you, too. Been thinking I owe you a listen. And I'm guessing you can put some, uh, better words together. Look, Ovid, I was working and took a break to call you about 2 a.m. and there was no answer." Her tone, though flat, has overtones of forgiveness.

Caught in the act. "I'm sorry, Karen. I was home, I had a drink, a couple, I guess, and I fall asleep. Never heard the phone."

"Sorry to get on your case, Ovid, but I know all about guys who have had 'I guess a couple of drinks' every night. I was married to one. I believe they're called alcoholics."

A punch in the face. But I'm far more upset with myself than Karen. Is she right? *Am* I overdoing it? Am I an alcoholic? This isn't the way this conversation is supposed to go.

"Are you still there, Ovid?"

"Keep talking."

"Look, I'm sorry if I jumped on you. I lived with alcoholism —my folks, my ex, you've heard it all—and I've seen a whole lot of what it leads to in the ER, but it doesn't make me an expert on the subject. There aren't any."

I can't respond.

"Ovid, say something, please. Let me know that you understand what I'm talking about. And that it's OK to talk about it."

"Karen, I guess I do drink too much sometimes. I don't think I'm an alcoholic. But I do understand why you're concerned, so I can't blame you. Can I ask you something?"

"Ask. But please don't make any rash promises. And don't expect me to make any."

"No, no. I just want to ask if we can start all over again."

"Ovid Kent,"—there was that full name thing again, a woman thing—"we haven't finished what we started in the first place. If you're not too busy catching up on your lost sleep tonight, how about coming by for dinner?"

Damn, she has just dissolved my self-doubt. I think about her invitation for exactly two seconds. "Sorry, I'm dining with a gorgeous babe."

This Karen doesn't miss a beat. "You're dining with two gorgeous babes. Miss April Knight and the elder Ms. Knight shall expect the pleasure of your company at six sharp." She talks funny. No wonder I like her.

"The even elder Mr. Kent shall be delighted to accept. Formal attire?"

"Socks required. Belay that, mate. I forget who I'm talking to. Don't be wearing *just* socks.

I'm nailed. "You've ruined my surprise," I say.

28.

Karen is no more than fifteen minutes away by the little motor skiff that came with my RICO-acquired *Bernie*. With no 101 rush hour traffic to stop me, I'm hailed aboard her craft at exactly six p.m. bearing a six-pack of Rolling Rocks, hastily borrowed from Ethel, plus a spray of cyclamen snatched from Ethel's starboard flower box.

"*Pour moi?*" says Karen, her head tilted and her hands over her heart.

"*Pour vous*, I reply," sticking the spray, little-boy-like, practically into her face.

Karen's fire engine red houseboat was converted from a steel-hulled channel tug half the size of the ones that usually ply the bay. I give it a quick look-see. "It's a pilot boat, if you're wondering," she says. "Got it because I found out it was born the same year as me. I'm sentimental that way."

"What's the boat's name?"

"Doesn't have one." How unsentimental. How does this woman's mind work? "C'mon, I'll give you the fifteen cent tour."

It's amazing what can be packed into four hundred fifty square feet. But it's all there. Living area, galley/dinette, bedroom, loft, head with shower. Cozy. Fixed topside are three kayaks—two singles and a two-holer—and a tandem bike.

When we get to the loft I see a girl lying on her bunk doing a TV Guide crossword. "April," says April's mom, "this is a friend, Ovid Kent."

April mumbles a hello without offering to shake my out-stretched hand. At first she looks through me, then she looks at me like I'm a truant officer. Distrust shows clearly on her un-formed eleven-year-old face. Her mother's looks are definitely there, if hidden under a sullen scowl. The big, wide-set brown eyes, the high cheekbones, the promise of full lips, and—when she finally drags herself erect at a look from her mother—Karen's slim structure and straight legs.

Hanging down her back is a thick braid, plaited—must be—by her mother. She's wearing a fleece hoodie imprinted "I'd rather be up a creek," a reference, I suppose, to kayaking. Might be a way to get close to this reticent young girl. By water.

"You like kayaking, April?"

Her flattened mouth says she's on to me. "Don't have any favorites. Mom, okay if I do some reading before we eat?" She gets a stern look from Karen before receiving a reticent yes. Then, still not acknowledging I'm alive, she picks up a Judy Blume novel and disappears.

Karen's face reflects a mixture of embarrassment and sym-pathy. "I suppose you're thinking April finds reading more fun than being with you." But there's no apology in her voice. "Please don't feel it's you, Ovid. She, even more than me, doesn't take too well to newcomers in her life. And especially mine. Especially if they're men. April will get used to you if you give her a chance. She's actually impulsive like me so she's had to learn to go a little slower."

"Like you're going with me?"

"Like I'm going with you. It's because of the mistakes I've made.

I don't remember inhaling. But I let out a huge breath. Does she see *me* as one of her mistakes? "Do you see me as one?"

Her shoulders go up. That's not a no, but . . .

". . . Hey, I got you your special martini fixins. In the freezer, right? New glass, too. "Pour yourself one and pop me a beer while I'm working and we can talk for a while. Then I've got a surprise for you." Karen's taking a different direction. And she's trusting me with the pour. Trusting me? She's stocked up for me. This is a very good sign. Even if the glass is half the size I like. But do not mention this, Kent.

I leer at her mention of a surprise. I'm leering a lot lately. Watch yourself, stupid. Twice a fool is at least once too much for any woman to suffer. I think I'm being tested. I'm pretty sure I'm being tested.

Reading the open book that is me—not hard to do—and punching me softly in the shoulder, she says, "No, not that kind of surprise." This is something you can sink your teeth into." I smile my most innocent mock smile. "No, no, we call it *dinner*," she informs me, punching my other shoulder.

We take our drinks to the fore deck to talk and watch another ho-hum sunset in paradise. "What's on your mind, Ovid," she asks, as we peel some shrimp. "Besides the obvious." But, before I can answer, she stops me.

"Wait, Ov, there's something I need to say to you." She looks directly at me. "I want to apologize for the way I jumped on you about . . . about the subject we were discussing on the phone."

This time I put a name to it. "Alcoholism. Specifically, *my* alcoholism."

"*Just* alcoholism. I'm not going to get on you about it and I'm not going to bring it up again. That's not the way it works . . . not the way I work. I had no business bringing it up before."

"Yes, you did, Karen. I didn't mind. You were concerned about it and, I hope, about me. Look, I don't think I have a problem, but maybe I do. You've given me something to think about."

"I want to say something else, too, Ovid, just in case you think I'm putting you off about certain things. Writing my phone number on your head wrap was about as subtle as the lovesick lover-boy act you put on with me. I was taking a big chance. It was a very un-cool thing to do, and I could have bought a lot of grief because of it, but I guess I can be as impulsive as you. If I seem a little inconsistent in my behavior, I hope you'll accept it instead of trying to understand it because I never understand it myself."

I look at her blankly. I don't understand it either.

"I take it from the look on your ruggedly handsome face that you accept my apology," she says, "so let me ask you again, what is really on your mind?"

"Thanks for asking, there is something else. A great big something else. It's a job I've taken on, some autographs I'm looking for. I told you a little about it before. I have a deadline and I'm reasonably confident I'll find them, but right now I'm stymied and I'm running out of time."

"What troubles you the most about it?

"This: I've got less than two weeks to wrap up the search, and you've got some vacation time coming, if I remember correctly. And frankly, my dear, I like being with you a lot more than I like chasing down leads that turn out to be one red herring after another. So, what's on my mind is this big job, but what's on my mind mostly is that it doesn't leave me enough time to be with you. I find that very troubling."

"Strange, Ovid, I feel much the same. I want more time with you, too, but we've both got a lot to take care of, mostly our work. So what happens with us will happen, I guess, if we just let it."

"Guess I'll take what I can get. You busy the rest of the week? How 'bout the rest of your life?"

For this I get a frown. "Please don't joke like that, Ovid. Busy the rest of the week? Not terribly. So we can see each other. For a few days anyhow before April and I leave. But this was the only time I could get off, and I promised her we'd go hiking and kayaking in the Sierras. And we're going to hit some used bookstores on the way there, that's how much she loves to read. I'm even pulling her out of school for the trip, that's how important this trip is."

"Maybe you can teach me some kayaking before you go."

"Why not? Presents an interesting picture. Can you breathe under water?"

"My mother was a sturgeon. Might have been her who busted my head."

"Ovid, I really do want to know about your mother. You've mentioned her before. And it's your turn to spill, remember? Anyhow, sturgeon roe, fire up that charcoal, I'm fixing that surprise. Remember, it's a *dinner* surprise. Try anything else and I'll have *you* fixed."

While I perfect the coals, Karen brings out two full slabs of her special baby back ribs that she's flour-coated and baked for finishing on the grill. Fifteen minutes later, the three of us sit down to the best ribs I've ever tasted. None of us speak again till the bone bowl is filled. Dessert is Ben & Jerry's Cherry Garcia— not the lo-fat—and minted dental floss.

After dinner, I slip myself another pour of gin, a short one. A digestive. I feel more than a little guilty because I sneak this in when Karen's busy on deck cleaning up the grill, which I realize should have been my job. April happens by. I ask her what she likes to read. She looks at me oddly, but her face softens enough to indicate she's heard me for the first time. She seems to get that I really want to know. "Harry Potter, of course, and I just started Tolkien. I'm going to read the whole trilogy."

"You know what a trilogy is?"

"Are you kidding?" she shoots back. "It's a threesome of anything. Like mom and you and me."

Nice word picture, April. "What's your favorite magazine? Seventeen?"

"Nah. Harper's. Mom gets it for herself, but she lets me read it even though it's got some bad words in it. They just don't usually use them in a bad way."

"Interesting take. Harper's is pretty heavy stuff. Some bad words, yeah, but plenty of good ones, too. And some big ones."

"Yeah, so?" she says.

"I've got an idea," I say. She seems interested, though her look of distrust has returned. I talk through it. "Take an issue of Harper's and underline all the words you don't understand. And then . . ."

"And then . . .?" She's all ears now.

". . . look up the underlined words in a dictionary and write out the meaning of each on a three-by-five card. Got that?"

"Are you kidding? That's a lotta work. Why should I?"

"Because I'll reward you for it. It's how I get beautiful girls to read." This brings an engagingly goofy smile to her face, the first suggestion of one I've seen. "Do what I just said and I'll pay you half a buck for every three-by-five you complete and show me. And you can take all the time you want. I'll, uh, I'll be around to check on your progress and deal out your earnings as they pile up. That OK with you?" Using a child to get to the mama. Shameless. But I do like this mama. And all's fair in you-know-what.

"Wow!" she says. "You'd do that? It could cost you fifty bucks, maybe more. You must really like my mom."

I accept the ca-chinging I hear in her head, but this is the second time this evening I've been caught trying to charm April. I recover enough to say, "A deal's a deal. You on?"

"You kidding? Sure I'm on. I'm gonna start right now. I'll have it done in a week, maybe two, 'cause how do I know how long you're gonna be around?" Then she flies past her mother on her way back to the cabin. "Ma, where's your latest Harper's?" she shouts, digging through the magazine rack. "Never mind, I found it."

"Who set her on fire?" says Karen, sinking into the deck chair next to mine to watch the rising moon bounce off the placid waters of Richardson Bay.

"Mammon," I say. I explain the deal, admitting that April quickly understands it to be a bribe that will buy me more time with her mother. "I hope you don't mind my having made April the offer?"

"You might have asked first, Ovid, but April doesn't miss

much," Karen says, tapping her temple. "You don't mind laying out that much reward money? How much you think I'm worth?" She nudges me in my rib-filled ribs.

I ignore her disgustingly salacious remark. "Can you think of a better way to fatten a kid's piggy bank?"

"No, Ov, I can't. Not a bad way to fill up her word bank, either. Earn while you learn. It's a nice thing you're doing, Mr. Kent. You may have turned a girl into a friend for life."

"Which girl might that be?"

Karen leans over and kisses her daughter's benefactor. Another of those barely-touching kisses, but somehow more meaningful, and she holds it a while longer. This is much better than that first kiss, that hardly-a-kiss. I'm not attaching any meaning to it.

But then I sense something larger, if not in the moment, then maybe in the sweet, sweet future. Does she feel it, too? It's something I haven't felt in years. Am I giving it more importance than it deserves, this simple—well, maybe not so simple—kiss? It was a kiss I'd like to be welcomed home with after a long day at work. Maybe it's time to change the subject. But not the object. Lust will have its way.

"That was a great meal, Karen. The way to a man's heart is through his stomach." My mock-bass voice suggests I invented the sappy epigram.

"The way to a woman's heart is through her kid," returns Karen. No pretense of humor.

I start to say something, but, detecting the look in my eye, Karen stops me.

"Ovid, remove that look in your eye. This is sacred territory." Hesitation. "Please?"

How does she know what I'm thinking? I wasn't even thinking about it till she said it. So what if I was. But I'll be damned if I let her know that. My forefinger goes to her pouting lips. "I understand, beautiful lady." I'm talking in a whisper now. "Tonight doesn't have to happen. I mean *it* doesn't have to hap-

pen. Not tonight anyhow because something else is already happening. What I'm trying to say is that I can wait for the other 'it.'"
I sense that I'm not altogether making sense and that I may just possibly be slurring a few words.

Karen is staring at me now with her mouth open. "Kent, you talk funny. The other *it*? Which *it* are you willing to wait for?" She's looking up into my eyes which may not be focusing too well. Hers are. "Is this you talking . . . or the gin?"

"This, Karen," I say, speaking through my gin, "is my heart talking. Is my heart talking too much? Maybe too loud?"

"Ovid?"

"What?"

"You're drunk."

"No I'm not. Well, maybe I am, m'love, but only for fifteen minutes. Such is the aftermath—the purpose, even—of a properly made martini."

"Ovid?"

"Yes?"

"Your martini went down over an hour ago. You're incorrigible, but . . ."

"Yes?"

"I . . . like you."

"You like me."

"I just said that." Her eyes are losing their serious intent.

"She likes me," I say. I like that. This is good. Like is good. "Is there a more pointed word you wish to use, a tad more strongish?"

"There is," she says, probably a little giddy from her own two —or was it three—beers. "But I don't fully trust my wishes."

I don't want this wonderful mood to go away. It's been a long time since I've trusted my feelings about any woman, but I'm trusting what I feel about this woman, my Karen. But, who am I kidding? Karen is not mine. Not yet. Maybe not ever. Am I in love? I ask though I know the answer. I am in love. I decide to sing. Out loud. "*I'm in love, I'm in love, I'm in love, I'm in love,*"—

as Nellie Forbush so fondly repeats in South Pacific—"*I'm in love with a wonderful girl.*"

I have improvised the 'girl' part, I inform her. She informs me that she is well aware that I have done so. "*There*"—as an even older Vaughn Monroe ditty says it, —*I've said it again.*

Karen is almost over the rail with laughter. "Ovid," she says, "chill out before your lungs wear out."

So here we are in a perfect limbo of, at first, non-expression, then, of warbled expression. Well, I'll just go with it, wherever it leads. What I've always trusted are my sharply honed instincts. They've carried me a long way. Professionally, if not personally. But if they've carried me astray occasionally, they've helped me find my way back as well. Now I'm thinking, where *do* we go from here? My sense of direction has always been somewhat lacking. Glad I don't have to walk a straight line. But what am I thinking, I do have to walk one. With her.

So where *do* we go from here? I suddenly recall that I slipped in that second gin after my second helping of those remarkable ribs, plus that little chaser. I slightly recall that my absence from the table, going for the second one, drew a downturned mouth from Karen. Good thing she wasn't aware of the third.

You're treading deep water here, Kent.

"I'm going to see my daughter off to bed and you're going to see yourself off to same. Yours, not mine," she says, still giggling.

I blew it. No argument. None allowed. Another of those "nice" kisses and I cast off, heading out of the harbor. The dizziness I feel now has only to do with what Karen had said about liking me. That's not quite true. The gin may also have something to do with it. Am I making too much of this liking business? Can this be the beginning of something more? Like love. I want to hear that "like" again. I'd like "love" more but I like that "like" plenty. I stop the skiff fifty yards out, stand straight up, turn and shout, "Did I hear you tell me you liked me, Karen?"

"Yes," floats her perplexed and muted reply across the water.

"What did you say?" I holler.

"I said yes. Yes, I like you." This time she says it louder, but not loud enough.

"Please say again," I scream.

"Yes, she cries, just a tiny bit louder, but with a conviction now obviously tempered by acute embarrassment.

"What?" I bellow.

"Yes, she likes you!" comes a matching bellow, this one composed of masculine voices from the weekly all-night poker game three houseboats over from Karen's.

I'm about to offer a macho reply to this surly bunch, but, before I can ungarble my words, I trip over the skiff's gunwale, which strongly resembles my bedroom's threshold, and I fall, butt over bandaged head, into the waiting bay . . . accompanied by the laughter of my poker-playing Greek Chorus.

It's a wet ride home. Uncomfortable, but not unhappy. She likes me. She *likes* me. I'm making progress.

29.

I jolt myself upright at 7 a.m. It's Sunday, a glorious tomorrow, the sun blossoming over the hills of Berkeley and Oakland. Karen's filling in for another nurse today.

I pick up the Sunday New York Times and fix my usual toasted bagel with butter and raspberry preserves, and slip into my faithful recliner. I'll devote these next three hours to the Times and the solving of its crossword and acrostic. If I dive deep enough into them, I won't have to think about . . .

"Where the hell you been these last few nights, kid?" demands the man materializing in my dew-laden deck chair.

"Who're you, my mother? Where the hell *you* been?" I snap back," visions of my Sunday ritual dissolving like cotton candy. But, though my head throbs from the previous night's debauchery, I'm feeling too good about being liked to feel mad. "Sorry, Babe, didn't mean to jump you like that. How you doin', man?"

"You sure got over your awe of me quick, kid. How'm I doing? You're the one who's supposed to be doing. And I happen to know you haven't been doing much since I last showed up."

"You're starting to nag, Babe. You on Milton Blackstone's payroll?"

"My orders come from higher up. Look, I was sent by the Boss to help you. And, yeah, even nag you a little. If you're not around

117

to use my help, that don't look so good. Not to Him, not to me. What am I going to do with you, kid?"

"Throw me back like old Doris?"

"Are you ready to go to work?"

"Yes, Babe, I am. I was never so ready. But I have this little problem, see?"

"I know what problem you got. You're in love."

"You are correct, sir. I may seem too old for love, several years older than you were when you checked out, but, yeah, I guess I am in—if it's not too strong a word—love."

The Babe winces. "Well, spare me the details, fella. What you do on your own time is your own business. Mine is to get you off the dime. Apply a little pressure from above, if you will. Why d'you think I'm on your case?"

"Because I've slipped off it, I know, I know. But I've come up with something I need to bounce off of you. Hey, you want a bagel or something?"

"You forget I can't eat that stuff? Got to stick to the swill they hand out on this side. By the way," says the Babe, "this Karen you're seeing . . .?"

"What about her?"

"I expected you to run into her or someone like her. The Boss's plan, remember? He's kind of a matchmaker in His own way. You and your Karen are both looking for the mother you never had. But you may have found something just as good as a lost mother. That's not His opinion, that's mine."

"Like?"

"Like, each other."

So the subject of love resides within the Babe. I like the man's take. "Very good, Doctor Ruth," I say, wincing myself at my unintended pun. "Who needs a shrink when I got you? You sure that analysis comes from you, not your Boss?"

He laughs. "You think the Boss has time to think about love?"

"Uh, I hope so," I say. Then I clear the dishes, clear my head, grab my legal pad and rejoin the Bambino aft for a cigar. He's back on the case. Fulltime, apparently. The Times can wait.

"Babe, if you know what I've been up to with my personal life, you must know what I've been up to with the Blackstone affair."

"You've been up to exactly nothing. A lot of runnin' in place."

"Not so. I've been up to plenty. But what you're saying is nearly right. I've *arrived* at nothing. Every lead I've chased has run me up a blind alley. I've gained an expert's take on the guy I'm looking for but I still have nothing and the clock keeps ticking. What's worse, Laura Cunningham has convinced me that John can literally die from the shock of losing those autographs. I do what I do mostly for the money, Babe, I admit that, but I don't want what I *fail* to do to kill somebody, to kill *John*. So just what am I doing wrong? Or what am I *failing* to do?"

"I don't know, kid. Maybe you're looking in the wrong places." He takes a last draw on his proto cheroot and flips it over the rail in an arcing trajectory that resembles one of his tape-measure home runs.

I go silent. I watch the stub hit the water and sputter itself out. I stare at it as it floats away, looking like a tiny turd in a huge toilet bowl. Then it just evaporates.

"Whadaya mean, Babe, I'm looking in the wrong places? My shrink pal, Eddie, suggested something like that."

"I don't know. It's just a statement." Now it's the Babe's turn to become pensive. We sit awhile looking at the fog rolling toward us, sliding under the bridge to spread itself like a down comforter over the waters of the bay.

The Babe speaks first. "You're looking for a guy who's got something to gain by selling the autographs. That so?"

"I was. I thought you were keeping up with me. The guy I'm looking for may have a stronger reason for wanting them. But what exactly are you getting at?"

"Just this. Maybe the guy wants to keep them. Maybe they mean as much to him as they do to Blackstone."

Hearing this theory for the second—or is it the third—time, I'm thinking an epiphany is just around the corner.

"That's very good, Babe. You and Eddie Diavalone think alike."

The Babe smiles back with the kind of cherubic grin he gave the fans after a round-tripper. I half expect him to tip his cap to my crowd of one.

"Maybe . . . the guy . . . wants to keep them." I roll the phrase slowly over my tongue. My thick head is finally taking this in as truth.

"So where you going with this truth?"

"Don't mind saying at all. You've just yanked my thought train off the wrong track. I'd been thinking all month about a thief with a thief's mind. But he may be a thief who isn't a thief. Not an ordinary one, anyhow. Just a guy who wanted to steal just one thing in his life. And he got lucky."

"Isn't that a real enough thief for you?"

"Yeah, Babe, but that's not a *thief* thief."

"Oh, now I understand everything. You want to start at the beginning?"

"You said it yourself, Babe, you hit it on the sweet spot . . ."

"Out of the ballpark?"

"Over the wall." The metaphor is quickly wearing thin.

"So what exactly does this lead to?"

"Maybe to the guy who not only lifted the sigs but is *keeping* them. It gives me a whole new take on him. Could be a collector who wants those sigs as much as John Blackstone does. Must have learned about them from John's story on the radio."

"So how you going to find him?"

This is Babe being the pitcher of his early years with the Red Sox. I never see this curve coming.

"Haven't figured that one out yet, Mr. Ruth." Something is gnawing at me. A missing piece of the puzzle. Something about the thief or the way he went about things at Overlook. Eddie had been perplexed in the same way. It'll come to me. "Hey, Babe, too bad we both can't go fishing."

The Bambino gives me a look. "If I could grab a rod, I'd grab a bat and get back to work."

❏

"Babe?"

"Yeah, kid?" he says, drawing life to a fresh stogie.

"I've got an idea."

"That's good, kid, you need one."

"It may be the answer to what's been eluding me." I hesitate, gathering my thoughts. "Let's say the guy really isn't a thief."

I have the Babe's attention. "Not your everyday thief, right? You're really taken by that thought."

"Let's say the guy's a collector who wants the sigs so much he takes a huge chance, steps out of character and becomes a thief for the first and only time in his life."

"You already said that. Keep talkin'."

I'm waggling my fingers, grasping at a thought that's slipping away. "There's only one reason for a guy to do that. But say the guy's *not* a collector. What if . . . what if the autographs have a *special* meaning for him? The same kind of special meaning they have for John Blackstone. I know guys like this.

They only want a sig directly from a certain famous guy for purely sentimental reasons. There are lots of guys like that. Like John Blackstone who would never let his sigs go. But maybe some other guy has a reason to want *the very same sigs*, the very same sheet of paper that John treasures just as badly as John does. And finds out at last that John has them. And goes after them. This is what I'm getting at. You follow me?"

"I'm ahead of you. Didn't John Blackstone tell you that's the very guy who snatched them?"

"Yeah, Babe, but how can that be? That was half a century ago."

"An obsession can't last a half-century? It can only get stronger in all that time."

"You actually think it was the kid who missed out on the sigs John got?"

"Why not? You got a better idea?"

My head starts bobbing up and down. The Babe's round head starts bobbing in rhythm with mine. We sit, silently, letting this new idea sink in. Ruth and Kent. A couple of bobble-head dolls.

"It's a stretch, Babe. A stretch to the limit. But if it is this guy, who is he? Where is he? Did he really appear out of the past and bust into John's room? If so, how do I find him?"

"Couldn't say even if I knew. Against the rules."

More silence. Then: "I got another idea, Babe."

"Shoot."

"I want to take you back to that day."

❏

The Babe pulls his chair a little closer after removing his camel hair coat. He's wearing a pair of blue slacks and a white sweatshirt with blue sleeves, the kind the players wore under their jerseys. He says, "You gonna try and hypnotize me or something?"

"I would if I knew how, but stay with me. I need to get your side of what happened that day in 1947. Recall it?"

"Yeah, sort of. You wanna know why?"

"You bet I want to know why."

"Well, I put out a ton of autographs in my time. But they was usually written alone on whatever I signed, not with a bunch of other what you call sigs. You understand what I'm saying?"

"Sure, Babe, keep going."

"Well, just getting together with Cobb and Speaker, especially that long after we'd played on the field, was so great. I mean for each of us and all of us. They were eight, nine years older than me, but we played against each other a lot in the years we were in the American League together. Sure, we were rivals, but we were good friends, too. Even Cobb, the S.O.B. The way he ran, I'm glad I wasn't a second baseman. Sharpened his spikes before every game."

I love these old war stories, but I wish he'd get to the point.

"Anyhow, though Speaker was nothin' special as a talker, and Cobb was a sonofabitch off the bases as much as on, I liked 'em. We had a lot in common. I'd still recall any time I broke bread with the two of them. That's my point."

"So that's why you recall that get-together in Cleveland?"

"I just said that. We'd been invited to an old-timers game before the Indians game. None of us could play a lick anymore, y'know? I was pretty sick and they must have been around sixty, maybe older. The Indians just wanted to introduce us to their fans. And we got a coupla bucks out of it."

"But what about that Saturday morning when John Blackstone came into the sandwich shop in the Hollenden? You remember that? You remember him?"

"Well, listen to me, kid, I'm getting to that. I only remember it because the three of us are together. It must have been between breakfast and lunch because hardly nobody was around. If it was crowded I never would have noticed the Blackstone kid."

"So what happened?"

"I'll tell you what happened if you can shut your yap and just listen."

I shut my yap.

"The kid acted a little strange. Didn't even say hi to us. Just stuck the sheet of paper on the table and mumbled a request for us to sign it. Which we did."

"Does this look familiar, Babe?" I hand him a photocopy of the autographed paper.

"Yeah, sure, I guess. Musta signed first, right there in the middle. Didn't leave much room for the other guys, did I? Even I thought the kid was lucky to get three autographs like that. I didn't sign a whole lot after that. Hell, I was gone a year later."

He stops talking then, maybe just to remember. He's immersed in the past. I want to keep him there. I give him a moment to fix those scenes in his mind.

"Babe, this is important. Nobody could treasure autographs from the three of you more than if they got them directly from you, right?"

"Right," I say. "Now, let's go back to that exact moment. OK, you're, all three of you, in the restaurant. John Blackstone has his sigs."

The Babe's eyes slowly shut. He sinks into his chair. "Yeah. The Blackstone kid mumbles his thanks and starts to run out. Probably to show 'em to his old man, or—because he's busting with pride—to someone, anyone, else."

"Yeah!" agrees the Bambino.

"Babe," I say, slowing myself down, "this next question is crucial. "Do you remember any other customers in the sandwich shop, any kids, anyone you actually notice?"

"No. Yeah. How would I know?" says the Babe. He closes his eyes and rubs his nubbin of a chin. "Wait a sec. The Blackstone kid runs into another kid, a fat kid, on the way out."

"Another kid, yes," I say. This has to be the kid John gave his concierge tickets to. Am I right?"

The Babe is almost in a trance now. "The other kid's about the same age. Blackstone shows the autographs to him. Then he points to us and shows the new kid the tickets I give him, then he gives the new kid some other tickets and half runs out the door to the hotel lobby. He leaves this new kid standing there holding his sack of sandwiches in one hand and a pair of game tickets in the other and just staring at us."

"This is great, Babe," I say. "This fat kid is the only one I'm interested in right now. So he asks for a set of autographs from the three of you, just like John Blackstone did?"

"No, that's not the way it happened."

"No? Well, then, how is it you actually remember him if you only saw him get John's tickets?"

"Because instead of rushing over for our autographs, which I can see he's dying to do, he spins on his heel and rushes out the door. That's why I remember him. Kids run to me, not from me."

"And that's it?"

"No. Just when I'm walking out the door to the hotel lobby ten minutes later, I see him busting through the street door again with a book in his hand. I s'pose an autograph book."

"And he never got even your sig?"

"Nope. I felt sorry for him because he was starting to cry but I had to run, I was late for the game."

"The poor kid," I say. Doesn't have the sense or the guts to ask a waitress for a pen and paper, and he sure as hell doesn't have the chutzpah to ask you for them. So, like the foolish kid most twelve-year-olds are, he runs back to papa to round 'em up and he misses the greatest autograph opportunity of his young life. But, you know what, Babe? You may have just confirmed the motive here. Not just the who, the *why*." I love you, man. And your Boss is going to love you."

We sit, silently, a while longer, smoking our cigars, thinking.

"I was just thinking, Babe. There must be a God."

"Getting around to that, are you?"

"Well, maybe. I mean, what else can account for you being here?"

"Good reasoning, kid. Kinda basic, though."

"Yeah, but . . ."

"Don't sweat it, Ovid. I am pleased to be of service. By the way, what's 'cuts-pah'?"

After I explain, he evaporates into the morning sunshine.

❏

Ovid? That's the first time he's used my name. Progress is being made here. But not on my case.

So I'm thinking over my lukewarm coffee. The kid bitterly regrets his loss for the rest of his natural life. At least, that's my theory. And it squares with what I've learned from John. This kid, by missing out on all three autographs, automatically becomes the one person who would kill for them. Well, maybe not kill, but steal. Anyhow, fast-forward to today, the kid maybe hears John on NPR or he reads it in the anthology. Only, the kid's now in his sixties like John Blackstone. He recognizes who John is and finally has a chance to get what he so tragically missed way back when and has coveted, obsessed over ever since. He figures he got cheated out of them back then, he deserves them now; they're his to take back.

But I've only got a missing person. Maybe impossible to find. The wind is slipping out of my sails. Even if my theory—*John's* theory—is right, my perp could still be in the Bay Area, maybe still in Cleveland, or anywhere between or beyond. But I'm guessing he's still alive because I'm also guessing he's our elusive thief and I have got to find him in two weeks. Make that ten days.

If I've guessed wrong, I'm dead in the water. Even if I'm right, I still have to find the man.

Where to start? Cleveland. My hometown. Don't know what I'll find, but the trail's got to start somewhere. First, I somehow dig up a name and some whereabouts. Had a feeling I'd be going to ol' Cleveburg. Old Man Blackstone thought so, too. He's amazingly sharp for his years.

Flipping my own stogie over the rail, the thought occurs: Don't be spendin' those big bucks yet, Kent.

❏

A minute later I phone Milton Blackstone to say I'm leaving for Cleveland. I have a lot to clear up before I take off. Reservations, packing, goodbyes. Karen! Christ, I miss Karen. I wonder how April is doing with her Harper's three-by-fives. Well, that's what phones are for.

30.

That evening, freshly laundered, I arrive at Karen's tug with a bagful of Chinese in hand. April's away at a sleepover. After chopsticking through our moo goo gai pan, we hit the deck chairs to lick the dessert I brought: lollipops. Karen reminds me that I owe her something.

"Which is?" I ask.

"An explanation about your Superman connection."

I promise I'll give it but I decide it's time to reveal Babe Ruth's strange entry into my life. With a leap of faith, Karen won't think I'm crazy. I tell her everything.

When I finish, she stares at me. She must be thinking I got hit on the head harder than she suspected. Then, without commenting on my revelation—which tells me she doubts me—she leaps to another subject. "By the way, Ovid, was that a splash I heard in the Bay last night as you were leaving?"

"I can't imagine what you're talking about," I say, blinking rapidly. She breaks into uncontrollable laughter. So do I. We take that evening apart scene by scene, roaring all the way.

Then she goes back to the thousand-yard stare she had when I finished my Babe Ruth story.

I knew I was risking my credibility, but I had to tell someone about the Babe, and I wanted it to be her. It's something I had to do; not lie to her, not hold anything back. About the Babe or about anything else. This, too, is Kent's Way. At least this is what Kent tries his damnedest to make his way.

"Babe Ruth, huh?" says Karen. "Talk about your strange men."

"I know how strange this must have sounded, Karen. But I want you to believe me about Babe Ruth. I need for you to believe me. I haven't lied to you. And I won't. I make that promise. It's not the booze, I promise that too. This Babe Ruth thing is really happening to me and it's something I have to ask you to keep strictly between us. You may think I'm crazy, but I don't want the whole world to think the same. I'm not crazy, I'm really not. I'm just a wonderful, lovable, good-looking, trustworthy guy you rescued from the E.R. A guy who, uh, likes you very much."

Karen fails to suppress a grin. "It's a stretch, Ovid. But, well, I'm glad you are who you are. It's just that . . ." She stops, her mouth held open in mid-sentence.

"Karen, what is it?"

"Okay, Ovid Kent," she continues, closing her mouth and setting her lips with determination, "I'll say it. Especially since I know that *you* know what a huge chance you're taking by telling me—or anyone, but especially me—this, uh, very strange story of yours. I know you don't mean to lie to me but, if you did, you'd hardly be the first."

Is she stalling? Where's she's headed? Do I want to know?

"You think I'm stalling, don't you?" she says.

"No, no," I lie. She reads minds. "I'm just waiting to hear what you have to say."

"Yeah?" Karen replies, "So am I." Then she hits me with a smile. "Well, here it is. And it has nothing to do with what you've just told me about your Babe Ruth because, honestly, I have to sit on those thoughts for a while. Anyhow, you ready to hear this?"

"Ready."

"You may think I'm crazy when I say it."

"Say it."

"Okay. I think I'm falling for you, you big lug."

Whoa, where'd that come from? Who cares, it came. She keeps a straight face after she says it, afraid, maybe, that any other face might elicit an answer she isn't ready for.

I don't have an answer. My jaw is open but nothing comes out of my mouth. I have the words but I can't find a logical order to put them in, so I return them to my jumbled mind. And my jaws to their locked position. I gulp. Deeply.

Karen waits a beat, then plows on. "Look, Ovid if you're being straight with me about this Babe Ruth business, if you'll be straight about whatever you tell me, I'll know it, sooner rather than later. I'm not sure how, but I will. If you lie, I'll figure it out somehow and—I promise you this—you'll never see me again." Lies are not my favorite things. Her response has to be coming from some dark place in her past. The edge in her voice suggests I shouldn't even think about going there.

"You can't imagine . . ." she starts to say, but I reach out and bring her to me and hold her tightly. She goes as limp as if lightning had just hit her.

"Karen Knight, did I just hear you say you love me?"

No answer. Her head nods up and down. She looks up at me to see how I'm receiving this.

I shut my eyes and breathe, just breathe, wanting to hold the sweet quiet moment forever. Then I kiss her and she kisses me back. This big lug is holding back a tear. Which he doesn't do too well. I'm home now, not looking around corners, not anymore.

Later she tells me, while we're still clamped together, that she can actually feel a huge hole in my heart. How come I didn't know about that?

"Ovid Kent, I have a question for you," she mumbles into my shirt.

After several beats: "Yeah, Karen Knight, I love you, too."

31.

I help Karen clear the dishes. As she's washing, me wiping, I steal a kiss and a nibble on the nape of her invitingly exposed neck. She turns, snatches my dishtowel and snaps it at me expertly, catching me squarely between the front pockets of my jeans. Must have been taking lessons from Bridie Cavanaugh.

"Arrghh," I cry, "Now we're *never* gonna have kids."

She replies by lassoing me with the towel, drawing me to her face and biting my nose. "The Marquessa de Sade, at it again," say I. Then she kisses it and makes it better.

"But that's not where it hurts," I say.

For an answer, Karen backs away and lays on another accurate nether snap.

❏

"Got your swim suit on?" she says, a little later. I nod. "We're going kayaking in the two-holer. It'll be cold at first but the action will warm you up quickly."

"What action?" I leer once more.

In five minutes we're in the water. I'm not sure I'm up for this. I need at least a houseboat under me to feel comfortable near any body of water larger than a hot tub. I have a hard time just lowering myself into the front slot of the kayak while it's at water's edge. Wasn't built for the damn thing.

Once shoehorned in, I feel unsteady. I'm certain we'll roll over any minute. This is decidedly not as natural as standing on the first tee-box at San Geronimo. But more natural than standing in a skiff while under the influence. I'm determined to tough it out.

We paddle out into Richardson Bay. The water is brightly moon-lit so we have no trouble seeing ahead. My only concern is staying upright. I'm not paddling so much as using the paddle like a tightrope walker to steady myself. But once we're underway, and the faster the kayak moves, mostly under Karen's strong, steady, experienced pulls, the better I feel. After awhile, we pull abreast of a tiny nameless islet, working our way around it to the side not yet lit by the rising moon.

"Want to check out the beach?" asks Karen, in a tone flatly devoid of innocence.

Assuming we're in shallow water, I begin to boost myself out of the kayak."

"Stop!" shouts Karen. But she's too late. As I rise above the kayak's newly-heightened center of gravity, it immediately begins to roll. I compensate by going against the roll, bringing the kayak sharply back the other way. In seconds it does a one-eighty flip and I, too shocked to take a deep breath before submerging, find myself upside down in water still over my head. Not having the air I need, my reflexes take over. I inhale while submerged, taking some water into my lungs. Then I feel Karen's arms circle me and, in seconds, the kayak, with me still firmly attached, is upright again. Spluttering and gasping for air, I promise myself that this business of standing in boats is going to stop here and now.

Karen, treading water, pulls the craft to a sandbar. I begin to breathe normally. We slide the kayak onto the beach and spread the towel that Karen had packed in a waterproof pouch. Then we lie back to catch our breath and gaze at the stars.

Karen props herself on one elbow and strokes my head. My soaked bandage is falling off. "Are you all right now, Ovid?"

I fling my stupid head bandage away with a flourish. "I could use a little mouth-to-mouth."

"That's what nurses are for."

We look at each other for a few seconds. I pull her down and kiss her full and hard on the mouth. "Seriously, thanks," I whisper. "You saved this klutz's . . ." She puts her hand over my mouth, then smiles mysteriously and gazes into my eyes.

If the air is cold, I hardly notice. I can feel the heat of her exquisite body next to mine as I yield to the transcendent way her hands and tongue begin to do their gentle exploration. Then I return the favor. I taste the salt on her smooth skin, the place behind her ear, her delicious neck. For the next twenty minutes the voyeuristic moon seems to lock itself into the night sky.

After our own locking, our arms remain around each other, knowing the moment will pass too soon. I don't want to let Karen go. We do not speak. This is a release, a first making of love. It needs no words.

❏

My kayaking courage restored, we make it back to the tugboat. "Nightcap? she asks, as I pull on my shirt.

"After that? No need."

Karen makes up a fresh bandage for me. For some time, we lie on her double chaise. She pulls an old afghan, redolent of her, over us. She snuggles into me, one leg lazily thrown over both of mine. Still no words, just an occasional sigh.

Then: "Aren't you going to need some tech support in Cleveland, Kent?"

"How romantic of you to ask, Knight. I'll have my phone and I'm taking my laptop. What are you getting at, my little lightbulb?"

"You're the bulb, Superman, I'm just the socket," she giggles.

Look you, you promised to tell me about that Superman thing? Spill!"

"No big deal, Karen. Here's the story. I'm Jewish, by culture, hardly by practice. My dad was born Bernie Kornfeld. He grew up in Cleveland with two other Jewish pals named Joe Shuster and Jerry Siegel, the two guys who created Superman/Clark Kent. Just when they were inventing him, I was born. You sure you want to hear all this?"

"Real sure."

"My mother, Clotilde, was a dancer, like you. Also a beautiful woman like you. She was on a spiritual and intellectual plane well above the earth my dad walked on, but my dad worshipped her. It was she who insisted I be named Ovid, after the Greek poet.

"My dad could never bring himself to stop her from doing what she wanted to do. She insisted on Ovid but didn't stop there, demanding a 'euphonious' last name to go with it. He hated it that his kid with the perfectly good surname of Kornfeld would have to go around with a first name like Ovid. She hated it that her lovely Ovid would be burdened forever with a last name like Kornfeld. So she pushed him until he broke down and changed our generations-old family name—it means what it indicates, cornfield—to Kent; legally, no less. She chose it because it had a high-class English sound to it. It tells you a lot about who she was.

"His pals, Siegel and Shuster, got a kick out of their buddy Kornfeld becoming Kent because of his new kid. Such a kick that they gave the surname to Superman's alter-ego. So, in a manner of speaking, I wasn't named after Clark Kent, Clark Kent was named after me.

"But my friends didn't nickname me 'Clark,' like you'd think, they loved to call me 'Superman.' And, of course, a lot of guys wanted to say they beat up 'Superman,' so I got challenged a lot and learned how to use my dukes pretty well. I did more fighting as a kid than the 'real' Superman ever had to."

Karen seems fastened to my words. I look over my shoulder at the past I'd been unreeling. "I thought my dad would never forgive my mother, not for the name change and certainly not for leaving him. She did run out on us, you know."

"I hope you'll tell me about that, too," said Karen, adding, ". . . when you're ready."

"We'll see," I reply. My mother was hardly my favorite subject. Her abandonment of us is something I never talk about. The feeling of emptiness and the loathing I've always felt whenever I think of her is something I've never fully understood, never particularly wanted to face. I almost got comfortable with it. Almost."

"And I almost forgot," Karen said, "that we were talking about some tech support for you in Cleveland. Do you need to look up names, search for suspects?" This was Karen, trying to ease my discomfort.

"I might. All of that. I'm sure I will. Why do you ask?"

"Because April's a computer whiz. Been one since her first Mac at age eight. One of the few things I can thank her father for. I'm thinking if you're busy you can message her to surf for information and relay it back to you."

"That's great. Outside of questing after rare books, I'm not much with computers."

"Well, I think she'll love it. It'll be another game to her. Like your vocabulary builder."

"You're on. I'll ask her. Thanks for bringing it up."

We share a single snifter of VSOP as we slip back onto the foredeck chaise. We're in a pensive mood. The night is darkening with the moon now snuffed out by the horizon. We take smaller and smaller sips, doing our best to stretch out not so much the brandy but this sweet moment, this mellow and memorable day. I hate having to leave on the next one.

Karen tells me she'll miss "this lumbering, this lovely, this hard-soft man, this rare mensch."

I laugh. "So continue your lovely critique." I circle my hand to generate more of her pleasing adjectives.

The Courvoisier, layered on our parting mood, is having its effect. Which is how Karen comes to break her "not-on-the-tug-boat" rule, and how her chaise comes to break its leg.

Before I leave, Karen says I'm pretty frisky for an old guy. I inform her that she's a damn good roll in the hay for an old broad.

❏

At 3 a.m. I putt-putt home, carefully sitting all the way, drunk only with my feelings about Karen. I perform a genuine leaping heel kick—just a single—on my gangplank. Time was, I could do a double.

"Good morning, Ethel, I love you," I croon. No can flies. It's too late in the night. Or too early in the morning.

Next morning I get a text from April. She's a third of the way through Harper's, highlighting the new words and writing out their definitions on three-by-fives, and I already owe her over sixteen bucks, and would I like to see the cards, and could I pay her now so she could get some stuff she needs for her trip?

"I promise to pay you when you're finished," I tap back. "That's so you *will* finish. Trust me," I say.

The negotiator in her speaks. "How about half now and half later?"

I quickly relent. "I'll have to break my piggy bank to pay you, Miss."

"Need a hammer?" she returns. Comes off like her old lady.

My plane leave in three hours. I shower, grab a bagel and throw a suitcase together. "You all packed, Babe?" I say, before my Uber arrives.

Silence. Oh, yeah. This Karen business is something he wants to keep at arm's length.

Right!

Part II.

Cleveland

A middle-aged man sits at one end of a tufted mohair Victorian sofa in his well-appointed pied-a-terre in the heart of a large Midwestern city. The man's several chins rest upon his tented, perfectly manicured hands as he stares, in rapt appreciation, at a montage newly affixed to his wall. The montage had recently resided in the bedroom of a San Francisco mansion.

A second man, clad fully in black, considerably younger, taller, strongly built and imposing, sits stiffly upright across from the man on the Victorian sofa. The second man, too, stares; not at the montage, but at the first man.

The first man obviously worships what he is looking at.

The second man, just as obviously, worships what he is looking at.

32.

Odd, to be coming home again. It feels like a million years since Cleveland *was* my home.

I loved the city. Still do. And continue to love and follow my Indians and Browns and Cavaliers. But my best memories are tucked away in my childhood years, before my mother disappeared to follow her creative muse west. Was that why I drifted west? I'd rather not think so. Was I looking for her or for me? Not worth wasting brain cells over.

The sight of the city triggers a buried thought as the plane begins its descent: I'll be in Cleveland for my dad's *yahrzeit*, the anniversary of his death. Which I'd have forgotten long ago if the funeral home, Berkowitz-Kumin, didn't insist on sending me yearly reminder notices. Maybe I'll take a short break and visit the old man's gravesite in Lakeview Cemetery. In Cleveland Heights. That's where I grew up.

❏

The plane banks out over Lake Erie, then turns for its glide into Cleveland Hopkins International. I can spot the old Terminal Tower, the symbol of my home town. And there are some newer, even taller buildings, Key Tower and the BP, that rose after I left. I pick out the Rock 'N Roll Hall of Fame, and the Cavs' arena, the football stadium and the Indians' Progressive Field, which they used to call "The Jake." The Municipal Stadium, where the photo of the Babe and John was taken, and the oldtimer's game played back in '47, has long since been flattened.

I shoulder my laptop and grab my ancient Hartmann overnighter. It's easy to spot. Suitcases, like dogs, come to look like their owners. Though it's not worth the twenty-five bucks I paid to stow it, I love the thing. Then I hail a taxi at the curb.

"Where to?" says the cabbie, evenly. It comes out more like, "Var toe." Strong Middle-Eastern accent.

"The Hollenden Hotel downtown."

"Can't," he replies.

"Can't?

"Why not?"

"Not there."

"What happened?"

"You want to know what happened?"

"I'm asking."

"Tore it down years ago. Put up an office building. Now the Fifth Third Bank. Ugly, you ask me."

The Hollenden, gone. Christ, how'd I miss that? That ain't gonna help me. I'm sure I've missed a lot about this town. But if this cabby knows about the old Hollenden, he probably knows a lot more about the rest of the city. He could be helpful. The DEA in me studies his placard. Nasir Ibrahim Nissam. "Nasir Ibrahim Nissam, can you take me there?"

"Sure, boss," comes the quick reply. "You got cash I take you to moon." I can see, through the rear view mirror, that he's grinning at me. "Hey, mister, you say my name just right. Even the 'Ibrahim' which is our 'Abraham.' You a Jew, ain't you?"

I figure it's just curiosity asking. "Yeah, does it show?" My nose is of normal proportions. No horns, no tail.

As if he hears my thoughts, Nasir laughs and says, "In my family we got a little everything. Sunni, Shiite, Christian. Even, way back, a few Hebrews, don't ask. You mix, it's good. I got a saying, 'If people move one country to left, the world, it will be a better place.' Hard to hate your enemy if you know him. But people with bombs," he adds, "them *I* want to bomb."

This philosopher is pretty good. But I need to get down to business. Though choked by the cab's tobacco odor, one I don't miss in California, I continue my questioning. "Nasir, do you recall a sandwich shop being in the old Hollenden?"

"Hotel was gone when I got here in '79. But, sure, boss, the Hollenden always had a sandwich shop called Moe's. It's still called that, still run by Moe George's family. His grandson Bobby run it now. You gotta talk to him. You want me to make an intro?"

"You're from Lebanon, right? And Bobby's your cousin." Nasir looks genuinely surprised that I people-read as good as him. The mirror shows me his broad smile.

"Call me Nate, boss. Everybody does. So how you know that stuff?"

"Call me Ovid, Nate. Forgive the typecasting but where there are sandwich shops, there are Lebanese, right? And where there are Lebanese, there are cousins, right again? One comes over, he brings the rest over. Like my people did at the turn of the last century. You got me pegged, I got you pegged."

Nate busts into a harsh, cigarette-informed laugh. "You got that almost right, boss . . . Ovid. You always say what's on your mind?"

"No, Nate, I just learned that from you. Listen, seriously, I'm trying to find someone connected to an incident that happened in that old Hollenden Cafe in 1947. You really suppose your Bobby can help me?"

"Actually, no, boss. But Moe probably can. Yeah, he's still around. Hangs out at Bobby's place, where else? You wanna talk to him? And, no, he ain't my cousin. But his people and mine both came from same village. Habbouch near Nabatiah."

"Yeah, Nate, I do wanna talk to him."

Ten minutes later we're downtown. Nate slips onto the short, narrow street called Short Vincent, once the colorful venue of Mushy Wexler's Theatrical Restaurant that catered to the town's best-known politicos, sports figures, lawyers, bail bondsmen and hookers. He turns right at East Sixth, turns right again, circling the bank, and pulls up to a cabstand next to it on Superior.

Before we enter the Fifth Third concourse I fill him in on my reason for the visit. He's intrigued that I'm looking for a thief. "I don't remember this town like I used to, Nate, so, if you're up for it, I'm going to skip the rent-a-car routine and hire you as my guide. Hey, Lebanese names usually mean something. Nasir means . . . ?"

"Guiding hand."

"That seals it, Nate. You're mine." He's got to be pulling my leg with that "guiding hand" business, something I'm sure he must do often.

"Plenty fine with me, Ovid," replies Nate. My cab, my badge, my choice. "You wanna know, I'm sick of the airport run. Nate will take you anywhere you want." He hesitates, then changes the subject. "Ovid. That's a Greek name, ain't it. Philosopher, right?"

"You know Ovid? He lived in the time of Christ."

"I didn't know him personally but I got a Phoenician cousin who did."

My turn to roar. "We're going to get along fine, Nate. Turn your meter back on and don't worry about running it up."

Inside, we pass a jewelry store, a kiosk hawking pashmina scarves, and several small boutiques. Tucked into the southeast corner of the bank building is a cafeteria-style sandwich shop that opens onto the concourse and, on its opposite side, East Sixth, not unlike the old Hollenden place did. The sign, painted in old-timey arching gold letters on the glass of the concourse window, says "Moe's Place." We walk in. Nate goes to find Bobby and Moe while I pick up some coffee and a cheese Danish and grab a booth on the Superior wall ninety degrees to the door on East Sixth.

It's a different century, a different building, but I sense immediately that I'm sitting at roughly the same sacred spot, where Ruth, Speaker and Cobb sat in the Hollenden Café all those years ago. And, if I figure right, based on what the Bambino told me, I must be facing the same direction as he had. If I've somehow channeled the Babe, maybe I can channel the scene of the autograph signing. I can almost see the young John Blackstone approaching me. And then another boy, fat and faceless, doing the same. I desperately want to see the second boy's face, as it was then and especially as it is now. And I desperately want him to be the boy I'm looking for. I'm waiting for him to speak to me, from then, from now. His presence is almost palpable. An involuntary shiver seizes me. Then I hear an ethereal voice whose volume is ramping up to normal.

❏

"Enjoying your Danish? I'd trade a four-bagger for just a bite right now." The voice comes from the booth behind me. It brings me back to the present.

"Ah, Babe, just the guy I'm hoping to see." I cover my mouth as I say this. Lunch seekers are beginning to walk in. I don't want to look like a looney, talking to myself.

"Back to the scene of the crime, are you?" says the Babe, popping up next to me. "You got the place right, kid. Got here often back then. Anyhow, I got a feelin' you're getting warmer."

"Was that the door the second kid used, Babe?" I'm pointing at the East 6th door.

"Yeah."

"Are you sitting about where you were sitting that day?"

"Close. How'd you know? I always sat at the same table when I was playing in Cleveland. For luck. Course, everything's different now."

I peer through the East 6th window. What I see is an old, still handsome, sandstone building across the street. I remember it from the years I lived here but don't recall its name. I make a mental note to check it out. Another hunch is forming.

"Excuse me, Babe, here comes my man, Nate, with the proprietor. I have to talk to him."

"Suit yourself, kid, I'm here for the duration," says the Babe, disappearing this time accompanied by a tinkling of bells and a dramatic hail of tiny stars. Showoff!

"Ovid, this is Bobby George, Moe's grandson. Bobby, Ovid Kent, a man who's asked me to help him find a thief who might have had something to do with this place when it was in the old Hollenden Hotel, even before Moe owned the shop there."

I shake hands with Bobby, make some small talk about my old Cleveland days, then ask, "How long did your grandfather operate the sandwich shop in the Hollenden?"

"For twelve years, till they tore the place down. When they rebuilt, he scored a lease for this operation. Then, when my dad decided he wanted to sit on a bench for the rest of his life instead of succeeding Grandpa Moe behind the cash register, Moe stayed on till I bought him out a few years back."

"So both your dad and your granddad are now retired?"

"Moe, yeah. My dad, no way. My father is a remarkable man, Ovid. He spent five years at Cleveland Marshall Law School becoming a lawyer. It was still just a small downtown night school back then, and all he could afford. Less than a dozen years later he was a judge. The bench he sits on now is the Sixth Circuit Court of Appeals. Right across the street on Superior," he says, pointing at a massive, low building just off Public Square.

Sharp, Moe's grandson. "I understand from Nate that your grandfather is still around."

"Last time I looked he was sitting over there in our back room with his cronies at the geezer roundtable. Don't tell him I called it that. I'd introduce you, but you can't talk to him now. The weekly meeting of the Little Lebanon Club has commenced. Moe's the Grand Poobah."

I peek through a half-open door next to the kitchen to see five men in their late seventies, early eighties, playing a highly physical card game, slamming down cards, drinking coffee from thimble-sized cups and all talking loudly at once in a language that can only be described as Lebanenglish. Bobby informs me they're playing Tarneeb. I don't ask him to explain it.

"Thanks, Bobby," I say. "You've been a lot of help. I'll get back to Moe later. By the way, do you know if he hung on to the records of the old Hollenden shop?"

"Grampa Moe hangs on to everything from the past. That includes the first nickel he ever made. Wouldn't surprise me if he still has records of the place that preceded Moe's."

I turn to Nate. "Let's head out to the Jake."

33.

John's framed scorecard of the oldtimer's game told me its exact date, June 28, 1947. It narrows my search for any material—a newspaper account, press photos, anything—that might identify, by caption or other notation, the kids in the background of John's photo taken with the Babe at the stadium. One of those kids could be—*has* to be—the one I'm looking for now. I have got to ID him. The Jake might have what I need. If not, then Cleveland's last remaining daily, the Plain Dealer, might.

Progressive Field, inaugurated in 1995, is one of the premier ballparks in the Majors. Today, nearly a month after the Indians' season has ended, the place, if majestic-looking, is as empty as a church on Monday.

At the executive offices I ask if there's a hall of fame or something at the park. I'm directed to a small alcove halfway around the lower deck.

Sure enough, the alcove sign reads "Cleveland Indians Hall of Fame." The place is packed with the memorabilia of past Indian greats: Cy Young, Nap Lajoie, Tris Speaker, Bob Feller, Lou Boudreau, Larry Doby, Leroy "Satchel" Page, more than two dozen others. I gaze questioningly at a bust of Speaker. His bronze eyes tell me nothing.

"Anyone home?" I shout.

"Out in a second," comes a croak from the rear. In quite a bit

145

more than a second, a wheezy wisp of a man in his seventies comes hobbling out to the display area. "Good morning, young man, I'm Harry Rosenberry. Been taking inventory. Who might you be and how might I help you?"

I explain.

"Well, you're in luck, son. We have quite a photo archive here. File 'em by the year, but not by the day or month. Got a cabinet for each year. Hoping to put 'em on the computer someday, but it's a day I'll never see. You're welcome to take a look-see. What'd you say your name was?"

"Kent. Ovid Kent. These are original photos, Mr. Rosenberry?"

"Well, they're from the original set of negatives. If a photographer gets a shot selected for publication, we try to get some copies or some of his rejects."

"I'll take that look-see, thank you, sir."

Rosenberry leads me to a room lined with file cabinets. He points out 1947 and leaves me alone. I spend nearly an hour scouring the 8x10s, looking for one that resembles the photo in the montage. Discouraged by the haystack nature of the search, and the mass of photos still unseen, I'm about to give up when I spot what I'm looking for. It's almost identical to the one I got from Blackstone but it's glossy and the background is more clearly focused. There's the Babe and John and, behind John, maybe a dozen other kids waving their scorecards for a signature from the Sultan of Swat. One of them may be the boy—the man—I'm seeking. Maybe the fat one third from the left end. My heart starts thumping.

Names, names, names. I hold the photo in both hands and shake it once, as if the motion would generate the name of the man who has given John such grief. Then, praying for names, I slowly turn the photo over like it could be the fill card for an inside straight.

No names. The back of the photo is blank except for the photographer's bold, rubber-stamped name and six-digit phone number in an oval. Hell, he's probably dead by now. My sigh is heard all the way out front by Rosenberry. "What's the matter, Mr. Kent?" he calls. "Can't find what you're looking for?"

I stuff the photo into my jacket before he returns. "No, Mr. Rosenberry. I was hoping to find names written on the back of these photos. Didn't press photographers usually do that?"

"Usually. On the ones they used in the papers. Or they stick the caption with the names to the bottom of the photo. But they rarely bother with the copies. Didn't tell me you were lookin' for names. You been through the PD morgue? The Plain Dealer. It might have the published originals."

"Not yet, but thanks for the tip, Mr. Rosenberry."

❏

P.D, Nate," I say, as I jump into his cab. In ten minutes, I'm facing the Plain Dealer's editorial receptionist. Don't know what her problem is but she greets me with a look that could freeze Death Valley.

"I'm Ovid Kent, private investigator," I lie, officiously. "I'd like to look at your photo morgue."

She eyes me with obviously practiced contempt. "Private investigator? Must be dangerous work," she says, dripping sarcasm. "Well, Mr. Private Investigator, this is not a film noir rag and we don't keep a 'morgue' anymore, we have a website that goes back only nineteen years. You do know how to use a computer, don't you?" "Is there anything else I can do for you?"

I don't say what she can to for herself. "Where, pray tell, is your research department, Ms. Stern?" A brown plastic nameplate sits on her desk. The name fits.

"Two floors up," she replies, turning back to her keyboard. "But they don't deal with the public." The word "public"—the hoi polloi—comes through a curled lip. "Only," she adds, "with writers, researchers, historians and other *professionals*." She never looks up as I leave without thanking her.

Two floors up, I'm met at a desk behind which is a shirt-sleeved man in Larry King suspenders. "May I help you," he says, removing his rimless glasses to wipe them.

"I'm Ovid Kent. Sports desk, Boston Globe," I lie again. "I'm writing a book about the last days of Babe Ruth and would like to check your archives regarding an oldtimer's game he attended in 1947 at the old Cleveland Stadium." He perks up. "Would you happen to have files of stories, maybe photos, used back then?"

"Why yes, Mr. Kent, we do. My name is Phil Levinson, with an 'i' in the middle, not an 'e'." Apparently he expects me to jot this down for posterity. "I'm the archivist here. Something of a sports historian myself," he says.

"And may I presume that your photos are identified with the names of the people in them?"

"Yes, usually. Depends. The whole caption is printed, including, if they're clearly visible, their names even if the names aren't used. They must sign releases and—"

"Right. So where might I find the original of this photo that appeared on the next day, the 29th of June? Or the releases that go with it?" I hand my purloined photo to Levinson-with-an-I-in-the-middle.

He adjusts his specs, squints at the photo, turns it over and looks up dolefully at me. "Excuse me, Mr. Kent, but this isn't a PD photo. See this six-point imprint in the corner? Says 'Cleveland Press.' I suppose you're aware that they—"

"—have gone out of business, yeah, thank you, Mr. Levinson," I say, deflating while taking the photo back. "Thanks, anyhow."

Damn! What kind of bum "private investigator" am I to overlook that imprint? Big-shot "sports desk man." The sandwich shop, the ballpark, the Plain Dealer. I've wasted an entire precious day.

"Find me a hotel, Nate," I bark, as I climb back into his cab.

"Relax, boss. Didn't go so well, huh?"

"No, dammit!" Nate takes me to the Shelbourne in Playhouse Square. I check in, empty my bag in the closet and dresser, splash some water on my face and head down to the bar. Happy hour's just beginning and the bartender's half asleep. I knock on the burnished mahogany and ask for a Gordon's Gin martini. By name. What I get is a dirty look from the startled bartender whose name tag reads "Chip."

"We have Gordon's in the well, sir, you sure you want it? How about Bombay or Tanq—"

"Gordon's, 'Chip,'" I snap, placing tight-lipped quotes around his name. "A double. You don't do triples, do you?"

Chip looks at me like he's doing the math on a triple tip. He dives into the well, mixes and pours. It tastes good, doing its job even if he wasn't. I wander over to the freebies cart and stab some dinner. A mess of pigs-in-blankets, dried out eggrolls and a few barbecued wings. It would all go down better if it were tossed into a blender with some rum. It leaves a bad taste in my mouth and ruins my perfectly good high. So I order another mart and nurse it for half an hour.

Afterward, in my room, I punch up Karen. I want to touch her. I have to settle for talking. "Hello, Nurse Nightingale, this is your impatient."

"Hi, Ovid," she replies. I love the way her throaty voice says my name. "I miss you, bookseller. I imagine you could use some nursely TLC?"

I skip a beat to let Karen's simple remark sink in. "Miss you, too, Nursely. Wish you were here."

"You a postcard?"

"If I was, I'd overnight myself to you."

We talk some more silly. Then about everything and nothing. We talk for an hour and a half. I unreel my fruitless day. She tells me about her plans for the Sierra trip with April.

Then: "Karen, I had a thought today."

"Just one?"

"Seriously. April said she could help me if I send her some data to process. I haven't been able to nail down the thief's name, but if I sent her an old picture is there some way she could update it so the people in the picture would look like they are today? That would surely help."

"I'll put her on."

Half a minute goes by. Then I hear April say, breathlessly, "How you doin', Ovid?" I like the way April says my name, too.

"I'm doin' fine, April. You taking good care of your ma?"

"The best. What can I do for you? Besides take your money."

I explain what I'm looking for. "Think you can come up with it?"

"Think so. My techy friend Ellie can. She sometimes Photoshops parents into old people. Plenty funny. Want her to try? And you're up to twenty-seven bucks on the three-by-fives." Pause. A question that sounds like a demand follows. "Plus ten bucks to Ellie for ID-ing the photo?" This junior agent will probably skim fifteen percent off the top.

"Right. I'll scan and send it right away."

"Gotcha. Gotta go. Bye, Ovid."

Karen gets back on. "I get the gist of what you were telling April. This girl thinks a lot of you."

"Which girl?"

"Both, Superman. Don't let it go to your head."

"Superman prays he can fly to Lois Lane as we speak."

"Soon enough. I'll let you get some sleep. It's well past eight here so it's near midnight there. You need some."

"Yes, I do. Could use some sleep, too." A groan from the other end. "Parting is such sweet sorrow."

"But part we must," says Karen. Say goodnight, my sweet Romeo."

"Goodnight, my sweet Romeo."

34.

Moe George is a big man, stocky, with bristly salt-and-pepper hair that makes him come off as a white Don King, the fight promoter—another local citizen, incidentally. In his mid-eighties, Moe looks twenty years younger. Bobby makes the introductions. Moe speaks in a loud rasp that can be heard across the room even if the place was packed which it isn't. His accent is there but almost undetectable.

"Sit down, Ovid, I've heard about you from Nasir. You got a name that's hardly Jewish, but you are a Jew, no?"

I'm getting used to this, so I roll with it. "*Nu*, you don't think 'Kent' sounds Jewish, Moe? Where'd your 'Moe' come from?"

Moe laughs. "You must be Jewish, Ovid, you got a sense of humor. You're a Jew with a Greek first name and an English last name. I got a Jewish first name and a last name that could be a first name and you're right, neither of 'em are my real name, which is Mourad Ghanem. 'Only in America,' as your wise old humorist, Harry Golden, used to say. I read everything he ever wrote. Is this not a great country? Now, what was *your* last name, Ovid? Kent, it couldn't be." I lay the Kornfeld on him. He nods his wooly head in smug confirmation of his own perspicacity.

Political correctness is not the old man's strong suit. Not mine either. "Glad you didn't mind when I made you for a Jew. You think I care about that stuff? I'm a Maronite Christian, some of my people are Muslim, mostly Sunnis, some Shiites, even. You, you're a Jew. Who gives a damn what we are?"

Then his big features become serious. "What can I do for you, Ovid Kent?" He snaps his fingers at his grandson and barks at

151

him to bring us some "real" coffee and a few slices of "Rose's special baklava." He acts like he still owns the place and Bobby, deferring, treats him like he does. Out of fear? Respect? Who knows?

Where do these Lebanese philosophers come from? This garrulous old man with the big hair and the booming voice is plenty okay. Bobby brings Moe's order. The thick, scalding hot coffee almost chokes me. But the sweet baklava is the antidote. It floats on my tongue.

"So tell me what you need, Ovid. I'll help as much as I can." I take him at his word.

"Okay, Moe. You ran the sandwich shop in the Hollenden for a lot of years starting in I guess it was 1951. Bobby says you kept every record of every transaction you made there."

"You want to see them?"

"No," I reply. "Those aren't the records I'm interested in." Moe shrugs and lifts his weathered palms.

"What I need," I say, "are the transactions, the books or receipts, for the sandwich shop that existed before you took over the place. For the year of 1947. Specifically, the day of June 28th. Moe, do you have those records, too? I'm looking for a signature, the name of a kid who was in the old shop that day. Would you possibly have those receipts?" By now my face is twelve inches from his. I suck in my breath.

Moe's eyes lock on mine but he's not seeing me. His mind is flipping back through the years. Then his heavy black eyebrows shoot up. "Yes, Ovid, I think I do. Don't ask why I save such junk. Especially since these records aren't mine; they belonged to Jake Solomon who sold me the old cafe. I was always concerned, though, that the IRS and the sales tax people might come after me if I didn't hang on to them. They're somewhere in our basement if the rats haven't got to them. Let's take a look."

I exhale. This could be the first break I've had. The name might be on one of Moe's receipts. Get the name, get the man. Maybe.

Moe moves well for someone of his years. His whole body seems to be held up by the wide black suspenders that give him a waistline just shy of his armpits. He sways his way down the rickety wooden stairs to the dungeon-like basement. The naked bulb hanging at the far end reveals a small mountain of rusted chrome stools and outlived kitchen equipment from the past half-century.

He clears a path to a wood-slatted bin in the corner. Standing over its old combination lock, he ponders a second, then spins the lock's balky knob left, right, left and pulls it open. How can he have remembered the combination after all these years? Tight ships are run by tight minds.

The receipts are stuffed into soiled canvas bags imprinted "Cleveland Bank," an outfit that must have gone out of business before I was born. Each bag is tagged with the year of its contents. He shoves several aside, then points to a few in the corner.

"There's what you're looking for Ovid. Take what you want, the hell with the tax people, they had their chance."

"Thanks, Moe. Just a few questions before you leave. Did Solomon keep his receipts the same way you did?"

"Yeah, you give the original of every tab to the customer, and spindle the carbon. Most tabs are for cash, but if a customer is staying in the hotel, he can sign and I walk the guest carbons to the hotel's front office for payment at the end of the day. Those days, most hotel shops operated that way."

"But if someone wasn't staying at the hotel and wanted to sign a tab?"

"Well, we had lots of outsider regulars. Mostly people who worked in the buildings around here. They could sign, too. There were no credit cards in those days, not till well after I took over, but we always gave credit to regular customers."

"And even a kid could sign a tab?"

"Sure, if I knew his old man. Of course, I kept those carbons because I had to do the collecting on them from the customer himself."

"Thanks again, Moe," I said. "What I'm looking for—if it's there—won't take long to find. See you upstairs."

I dive into the bag marked '*47*. It had been packed with rubber-banded carbons, but the rubber bands have long since disintegrated and the checks are now a jumble of faded green rectangles with white borders, browning at the edges and beginning to crumble. Each check has a little spindle-hole near the middle.

I dump the checks onto a large, deeply gouged butcher block table and spread them for sorting by the month. I find the June tabs and fan them out for further sorting. I come up with about forty checks dated with the magic numbers "6/28." The 28th of June. Most carry no signature, indicating they're cash duplicates, no sig required. I'm looking for a kid's signature, a kid who ran out the Sixth Street door and was able to return within five, ten minutes. A kid whose father therefore likely worked in a nearby building, likely enough the one across Sixth. It's a long shot but the only one I've got.

There won't be one signed by John Blackstone for his father to pay later. Nor for Ruth, Cobb, Speaker or any of the other old timers. They all stayed at the hotel, and anything signed by them would have been walked to the hotel's front office that same day for payment. I clear off the no-names to inspect the dozen or so remaining.

I come down to two checks, one or the other of which, I'm certain, is what I'm looking for. But who am I kidding? I'm not certain at all.

The first has a juvenile scrawl written so large it has to turn and run halfway up the right side of the paper. Underneath the scrawl is a small, neatly lettered first and last name, likely printed by the cashier on duty that day. Under that, in the same small hand, is another name, same surname. First printed name has to be the son, beneath that, the parent, the "regular." The second check is signed in a slightly smaller and neater hand, but definitely that of a youth. It, too, has a printed-out name below it

and, below that, another. Another likely son-father pair.
The only son-father pairs:

| *Billy Gerson* | *Harley Thornhill* |
| *Harold Gerson* | *T. Gordon Thornhill* |

Are one of these my man? Do I have the name of the boy who
later, as an aging sixty-something, has come, by nefarious
means, to possess John Blackstone's most precious possession,
the loss of which is killing John by degrees? Or do I have another
rotting red herring?

My hands coated with basement scum, I haul myself out of
Moe's cellar and ask Bobby for a phone book. I find two William
Gersons. Probably can't reach any of them during the day. But
no Harley Thornhill or H. Thornhill. No Thornhill at all. Moved?
Unlisted? Dead, maybe? I'll put Leo Cavanaugh on it. Leo has
nothing better to do, right? I ring him up.

❏

"Lieutenant Cavanaugh here."

"How they hangin', pal?"

"A little to the left. I must be a lemon, Ov, 'cause I think I'm
about to be squeezed."

I've heard that one before, too. "Got that right, flatfoot. I'm
in Cleveland. Need some quick background on any Billy or
William Gerson who lives here. Also, a Harley Thornhill, possibly unlisted. Harley Thornhill's an unusual name so maybe you
can check other cities for him. Need their ages, plus a phone
number and address for Thornhill. And a recent photo if you can
find any. Any of 'em might have died or moved away."

"Maybe you'd like me to come out there and make the collar
for you, too? I'll get back to you, ducks."

"Love ya, mean it, Leo."

Meanwhile, I'll follow up on the Babe's recollection of seeing the boy run out the door that led directly to the street. To—my earlier hunch—a nearby building? I pocket the two old sandwich shop tabs, thank Moe and Bobby, try to pay my bill, am graciously refused, leave and dodge a few cars while jay-walking across East Sixth to . . . I see its name now, chiseled into the arched entry: Leader Building.

35.

The Leader Building is a faded '20s neo-classic with a vaulted, high-ceilinged lobby and well-worn marble floors. Its elevators retain the scrolled brass-and-wood-paneled elegance of the building's early years. The small management office, Number 410, is overseen by a painfully thin woman, probably in her sixties, her back to me. I notice a dormant computer on the rear counter next to her, but she's typing envelopes on an old IBM Selectric. I walk up to the counter in front of her desk. "Plain" would describe her perfectly. She looks like a Gardner Rea cartoon. Even from the rear I recognize her piped suit jacket as an expensive Coco Chanel, old and out-of-date even if Chanel is never considered out-of-date. Only old money can dress like that and get away with it.

The typewriter I find encouraging. Any building's management, still old-fashioned enough to use one, likely keeps its records in the same old-fashioned way, hopefully going back long before the '40s like the Leader itself. Her desk plate reads "E. Tarkoonian." She doesn't seem to notice me, though I hover over the railing in front of her desk, shifting my hundred-ninety-five pound bulk for fully half a minute. The four-foot-high railing is as plain and wooden as the woman herself.

"Emily?" I say, at last to get her attention. She looks like an Emily.

The woman spins in her chair and jerks her head up to peer at me through huge, incongruously pink-and-polka-dot-framed

157

glasses. "How did you happen to know my name?" she says, a surprised look on her face.

"Educated guess. I'm Ovid Kent," I say, handing her my card. My mind had gone through Ellen, Elaine and Ernestine, and had almost opted for Edna. But Emily it is. How perceptive, Mr. Kent.

She glances at my card, a strange smile wafting across her face. "What is it you'd like, Mr. Kent?"

"Ms. Kartoonian, I need . . ."

"Tarkoonian," she corrects me.

Sorry, Ms. Tarkoonian. I *urgently* need some information about a man who was a Leader Building tenant back in 1947." Then I add, leaning in with a touch of drama, "The information can possibly save another man's life." Finally: "Is there a manager to whom I may speak?" Good grammar might count here.

She appraises me, her head cocked a good fifteen degrees to the right. "Please be seated, Mr. . . ." She looks again at my card. "Mr. Kent." Then she lopes over to the inner office door, raps ever so softly, and walks in before she gets a reply. She's wearing pink Crocs that match her glasses.

I hear some muffled laughter behind the door. Then, a moment later, she emerges, straight-faced, and waves me past her with a "Please enter, Mr. Kent."

I find myself facing a tall skeleton who is Emily with a bad comb-over that might look passable if it weren't dyed a solid black. His desktop is clear except for an old calculator, a phone and a fat Rolodex. Mr. Bones looks at me in the same appraising way Miss Emily had. He puts out a limp hand and introduces himself as "Emil Tarkoonian, CEO and co-managing partner, along with my sister, of the Leader Building Group." Emil and Emily. Twins? Isn't that cute. And the receptionist is his partner? In the Group? It's not just a building, it's a group? I'd been right about the old money. Inherited likely. I'd bet that neither of the Tarkoonians is married. And that they live together. My hunches are usually right.

"You can see, Mr. Kent, that my sister takes care to protect me. Rarely allows anyone past the bulwarks. But she seems to have been touched by the fact that someone's life may depend upon your finding a former tenant of ours. I'm curious; whom exactly is it you're seeking?"

"Two men, actually. One is a Harold Gerson. Also, a T. Gordon Thornhill. Information I have suggests they may have been tenants here in 1947. Do your records go back that far?"

"They most certainly do, Mr. Kent," replies Tarkoonian. "Our records, I'm proud to say, survive from when my grandfather built this building in 1913. The family almost lost it in the Great Depression, but we hung on, and now it's the flagship of a nationwide fleet that contains many—shall we say—larger ships."

I'm impressed. Especially since Tarkoonian's undertaker suit is two inches short in the legs and so shiny I can practically see my reflection in it. Whatever old money is, it apparently doesn't get spent like yours and mine. The decidedly eccentric Tarkoonians—I learn later from Nate that they own half of downtown Cleveland—are something of a philanthropic living legend in the Forest City, and are—are you ready for this?— unmarried and live together in the most opulent residence—the old Van Swearingen mansion on Shaker Lakes—in Shaker Heights, a positive trove of Cleveland's most ancient money. You oughtta be a detective, Kent.

"We keep those records in the attic, Mr. Kent. Shall we take a look?"

"By all means, sir." I follow him out of his cramped quarters. With new respect for Emily Tarkoonian, I nod my obeisance to her before her brother and I clop down the marble hall toward the spiffy elevators.

The eight-foot high carved oak double-door entry to the "attic" actually says, in gilded letters, *The Attic,* beneath which are the words *World Headquarters, The Tarkoonian Group.* I'm thusly prepared for the awesome layout that awaits us on the penthouse operations deck of the Tarkoonian flagship. A young, willowy Eurasian woman is languishing behind a long, black-lacquered desk whose curves are as well-formed as hers. She sits up when she sees her boss.

"Good afternoon, Mr. T," she says, in a voice that would melt chocolate. "Shall I inform anyone you're here?" I glance over her comely shoulder through the north-facing floor-to-ceiling windows. They reveal a roiling Lake Erie, spewing waves over the seawall, a harbinger of the North Coast winters I've tried to forget.

"Don't bother, Tamara," Tarkoonian replies. "We're just heading back to storage. We walk through a pair of massive zebrawood doors into a posh bullpen that occupies most of the premises. This is surrounded by luxurious executive offices, one larger than the other.

I'm ready to ask Tarkoonian if he needs a chief librarian.

We continue past a repetition of *Good afternoon, Mr. T* coming from the open doors of the exec offices. Their occupants have obviously been warned of the Mr. T sighting by the Tantalizing Tamara. He first-names each before we stop at a vault-like door marked "O.R." Emil notes my puzzlement.

"It's not an operating room, Mr. Kent," he says, with a cadaverous grin. "'O.R.' stands for 'Obsolete Records.'"

Tarkoonian, the unassuming empire builder, pulls out a janitorial-sized ring of keys from a retractor on his belt. He finds the one he's looking for by feel, then admits us and flips on overhead floods that reveals dozens of highly polished, age-old oak file cabinets each worth twenty times its cost on eBay.

The cabinets are marked with the names of older Tarkoonian-owned buildings and the years their tenants occupied them. Emil walks down the rows, looking neither right nor left, stopping, instinctively, at a file tagged "Leader '47." Using another key and with some serious effort, he pulls open the drawer labeled "G-L." The "G" files reveal no Gersons. Worse, neither does "S-Z" yield any Thornhills.

Another dead end. I let out a silent scream. Then a pensive look comes over Tarkoonian's long face. His long fingers drum on a cabinet top. "That name sticks with me," he says.

"Which one?"

"Thornhill." His eyes widen. "I remember now. Patterson, Thornhill & Cline." My eyes widen. Tarkoonian opens the middle drawer, "M-R," and riffles back to a file labeled with the names he's just mentioned and studies it for a minute. "This firm occupied half the seventh floor during the years 1938 to 1976 when they disbanded. I clerked here for my father during those later years. In the '70s, T. Gordon Thornhill was Patterson, Thornhill's managing partner. They specialized in patent law or what is now called Intellectual Property Law. What do you need to know about Mr. Thornhill, Mr. Kent?"

All the while Tarkoonian has been talking my smile is growing. I've found my name. Now all I have to do is find my man. "Nothing at all, Mr. T. Just by locating that file, you've told me all I really need to know. I thank you, sir. And please extend my thanks to your lovely sister, Emily, as well."

"Emily?" says Emil, looking smug. "My sister's name is Eleanor. Whatever gave you the idea her name was Emily?"

Is this man putting me on? Well, if he isn't, the old broad was. Eleanor. Not even one of my first choices. How prescient, Kent.

I thank Emil again and walk out laughing. With him and his sister. And at myself.

36.

Harley Thornhill has to be my man. Is. If he isn't, I'm screwed. If he is and I can't find him, I'm screwed.

I massage the scene the Babe laid out for me, turning it into a scenario I can believe in and chase after. I drift my mind back to that Saturday in June at the old Hollenden Hotel. At T. Gordon Thornhill's request, his son Harley leaves the Leader Building and crosses East Sixth to the Hollenden to pick up lunch for the two of them at the sandwich shop. The son grabs the food, then, like John Blackstone, spots Ruth, Cobb and Speaker sitting there, perfect targets for an autograph. Having read the morning's sports pages, and with baseball knowledge beyond his twelve years, he not only recognizes all three, he fully realizes how unique it would be to capture their famous sigs together. He's so excited he almost wets his knickers. Panicking because he has no paper or pen, he makes the foolish decision to rush back and get them from his father. When he returns he sees the Babe walking out the opposite door. It's too late. He gets *no* sigs. He's so crushed by his lost opportunity to nab all three that he starts running out of the place, literally running into John Blackstone who had, minutes before, secured all three sigs and was still there staring at them.

The proud Blackstone sees an opportunity to display not only his newly acquired treasure but the fabulous box seat tickets the Babe had also given him for that afternoon's old timers day. Harley, enraged and angry with himself, is about to snatch the loose-leaf sheet of sigs. They should have been his! But John surprises him by holding out the concierge tickets to him. Harley takes the tickets which will put him at the game today. This sets the stage for the photo of the Babe with John, and with Thornhill as the fat boys in the background of the photo.

Harley shows at the game. But he'll never own the autographs of these gods of the Cooperstown pantheon. Never. He took the tickets from the stupid-looking kid whose mouth hangs open when he talks. But he hates him for having the sigs he'll never have.

What a thought! No good deed goes unpunished. The image of Harley Thornhill, the thief, the architect of John's abject misery, has been hanging on John's wall all these years, as if to mock John while awaiting his chance to rob him. It's fitting together like a jigsaw puzzle. But did it actually happen this way?

Don't get too carried away, Kent.

The way young Thornhill's mind works—malfunctions—he will focus upon his tragic loss much as John Blackstone revels in his gain. Harley Thornhill will be obsessively and uncontrollably jealous of the Boy Who Got Ruth's, Cobb's and Speaker's Autographs, *all together,* for the rest of his natural life.

But what can Thornhill have been thinking? Can he actually have believed that he deserved or had some kind of right to what John Blackstone had so serendipitously acquired?

It's time to find out, to find Thornhill and face him with this terrible thing he's done to John Blackstone. And it's time to retrieve the signatures. That's why you're here, Kent. That's why you're being paid the big bucks. So do it! Be findable, you bastard!

But what am I thinking? Thornhill's not a kid collecting autographs anymore. He's probably collecting Social Security. You want this to be easy, Kent. You finally have a name but you have no whereabouts, no picture of who you're dying to facet.

And there's no Thornhill in the phonebook, no clue where to find him. I may no longer be on square one, but I'm not much past square two.

Then, just like in the movies, my phone trills its "Für Elise." Leo Cavanaugh, calling to connect more dots I pray.

"Kent, what god you been praying to? I've got your perp. His name is . . ."

"Harley Thornhill. Tell me I'm right."

"Nice work, Ov. You're right."

"Now tell me you found him still in San Fran?"

"No, of course not."

"New York? Cedar Rapids? Dubai?"

"Much better. You ready for this? Cleveland."

"Ho-lee shit! Lieutenant Cavanaugh, do not be kidding a kidder."

"You sound like my mother-in-law. But this I would not kid about, kiddo. Talked to a few pals. Looked under a few rocks where you're not welcome to look. Got more than you could hope for."

"Which is . . .?

"Thornhill and another guy, a Richard Harmony, made a trip to San Francisco earlier this month Harmony's an ex-con. The dates fit. They arrived five November and left eight November. I'll send you a copy of their E-ticket. Also, pally, even without my sources I remembered that you'd checked Blackstone's phone bill but of course you didn't have the latest calls. That's because the latest bill hadn't come yet. So I check and there it is. A call from your suspected perp. And another going out to him."

I blow out a huge breath. "You're one good looey, Leo."

"I'm gooder than good, Ovid. Wet the point of your pencil stub, I'm gonna give you Thornhill's whereabouts. He's in downtown Cleveland at a place called the Southington."

Another exhale. My ears are lying to me. "Really, Leo? You didn't make this up? I could piss out my window and hit it from where I'm staying. With you and God on my side, this loser can't lose." Sorry, Babe, I had to leave you out.

"God's on your side? You heathen, your presence in a temple would bring its walls down."

I jot down the unlisted phone number he gives me and stare at it a full ten seconds before replying. "Leo, you are indeed fantastic. You made only one mistake. They must have arrived on four November, not five. The break-in was on the fourth."

"Ain't no mistake, Ovid. I know when the break occurred. I said five, I meant five. You figure it out."

I figure it out. I don't want to believe what I—and Leo—now know. "I owe you big time, buddy. Taking you and Mary Ann and Bridie to Jardiniere for dinner soon's I get home. That is, if this thing goes down right. Thanks again, mon frere, and give your ladies a passionate kiss for me."

37.

Things are falling into place. A strange place. Obviously, if Thornhill and his friend arrived in San Francisco the day after the theft, they couldn't have committed it. They could only have come to pick up the loot. Which leaves only one logical suspect.

The goddamn butler did it?

If I were writing a mystery . . . never mind. I'll deal with Thomas later. There must be another explanation. I sure as hell hope there is. Not for Thomas's sake, for the old man's.

So Harley Thornhill lives at the Southington. An unbelievable stroke of luck he still lives in Cleveland at all, but at the Southington of all places. Could be it isn't such a coincidence? The Southington is also near the old Hollenden. Can that be why he lives there? To be near the source of his obsession? Too weird. I'll leave that stuff to Eddie. Could be, too, that the Babe's Boss is involved. Well, thanks obsession, thanks Leo, thanks Babe, thanks, Boss.

Have I missed anyone?

❑

Well, now I can stroll over to Thornhill's digs, snatch the goods, catch a westbound redeye and maybe be home in time to see Karen before she and April leave for the Sierras.

Cancel that. Counting chickens.

My impulsive nature tempts me to head for the Southington immediately. But, for once, I'm going to move with Due Deliberation. I have the upper hand now. I know exactly where I'm going while Thornhill has no clue I'm coming. If I want to use it. But I have to be absolutely certain I have the right man and I still don't know what he looks like.

I'd call Thornhill just to make sure he's in, if I didn't think his Caller-ID would ruin my little surprise. On the other hand, if I bust in and he's there, what if he has an apartment full of guests? How can I quickly identify him? He could get the jump on me. *I need that old photo updated.*

For the first time in the past three weeks, I have the luxury of time. Of hours, even days. And I'll savor the confrontation all the more if I wait a day or so. Besides, this'll give April time to have the photo updated.

And—where does this come from in the midst of my Capture-the-Flag frenzy?—tomorrow is my dad's *yahrzeit*. I will pay him that promised visit.

I stick to the Shelbourne for dinner. Head too filled to seek better. After washing up, I grab the old montage photo to have the front desk scan it so I can send it back to April. With any luck, she can have her friend Ellie email the Photo-shopped update back within a day. There's nothing more I can—or care—to do for now. The big hand and the little hand suggest that I stroll into the bar.

38.

"Hi, Mr. Kent, the usual?"

"Yes, Chip, that would be nice."

"How about a double?

"That would be nicer."

"No, it wouldn't," says the Babe, sitting, suddenly, two stools away. His voice is bland, but his eyes are piercing mine in the mirror behind Chip.

"Make that a single," say I.

"A single?" says Chip. "I thought you said . . ."

"I did. Make it a double, what the hell."

The Babe's watermelon of a head is wagging. I cave.

"A single, Chip, that's it. Make it a single. That is final." The Babe is here to help me, to go to bat for me. I'll behave.

Chip, thoroughly befuddled, sets the Gordon's bottle—which he now keeps in his freezer for me—some vermouth, a frosted glass and a twist of lemon on a napkin in front of me and walks away. A large-boned woman who looks like the head of the hooker's local slips onto the Babe's stool. He doesn't blink. She looks like she's sitting on his lap. "Excuse, me, I say, "that seat is taken."

"It certainly is, big boy. Care to buy a lady a drink?" I flash her my ancient DEA creds. She leaves. Quick.

"Nice move," says the Bambino, pretending to brush off the remains of her.

I raise my self-poured—to the top—single to the big man and say, "Here's to you, Babe. Always knew you had the power."

"What was that you said, Mr. Kent?" says Chip.

"Nothing, Chip. I'm just talking to Babe Ruth about his power." What the hell made me say that?

"You do that, too?" Chip replies. "I always talk to the Babe. Mantle and Aaron, too. You can have your .400 hitters, I'll take the long ball every time."

"Right," I say. To the Babe I say, softer, "Mind sitting dinner with me? I need to fill you in on what's been going on."

He looks at me with a smile. "By now you should know you don't need to fill me in," says the Babe. "I know what's going on. You may think it's luck or coincidence, and you may be right, but I got a feeling the Boss was feeling a little sorry for you." As we stroll toward the dining room, he says, "I can't eat, but I can dream about downing the steak you're having."

"Steak?" Is that what I'm having? Can you make me eat steak?"

"Yeah, since you ask. I got mysterious ways too."

"Well, Babe, I love a New York Strip. But eating a steak anywhere but a steak house is usually a disaster. These continental restaurants tend to smother theirs in sauce."

For once, the Babe looks like he's learning, not teaching. "I'll try to remember that, Ovid. So try the long bone veal chop. But you want the real truth? Nothing's going to be good here. Chain hotels serve crap."

I ponder the Babe's perspicuity. "You do have a way with words, Mr. Ruth. Can we talk about the case?"

"I'm listening, kid."

"This is not going to be easy, Babe. When I talk to you in a public place, I look like I'm talking to myself."

"How about I ask you yes-and-no questions? You OK with

that? You can just nod your head. I thought we been through all this before."

I nod my head. Then I order the veal chop and hate it. Tastes like a catcher's mitt. I send it back for a chicken pot pie. Big mistake. Tastes like a catcher's mitt. Ready to change hotels, or at least dining rooms, I pass on the dessert and invite the Babe up for a cigar.

❏

"So you think you got your man?" says the Babe, lying on his back, ankles crossed, plotzed in the middle of my king-sized bed. He's taking huge drags on his bogus cheroot. He's the picture of total relaxation. I'm not.

"Let's just say I don't want to believe I haven't got my man. The guy—Harley Thornhill—lives in a condo just a few blocks from here. I don't know what he looks like, but I should be getting an updated photo of him any minute now."

"So that means you knock on his door tomorrow?"

"Yes. Or the day after, latest. That's why I'm here, right?"

"What'll you do with him once you nab him?"

"Not sure. Maybe nothing. Milton Blackstone only wants the return of the sigs. It's sort of a 'don't ask, don't tell' deal. Hit and run, you understand?"

"I guess so, but what if your guy doesn't want to cooperate?"

"That's easy. I grab the montage, hit him and run. Kidding, Babe. The guy's in maybe his late sixties. But what *do* I do with him? Fact is, I don't know what I'll find and I don't know what I'll do when—and, okay, *if*—I find it. But I have found him, I know I have, thank God."

"Glad you acknowledged that, Ovid. Don't want to piss the Boss off."

"The guy's got an accomplice, too. That's important. Hopefully, only one. Could complicate things. Got to let it all unfold at its own pace. I'll know what to do when it's time to do it. Or I think

I will. Hey, Babe, not to change the subject but will you be insulted if I ask for a little privacy?

"Nah. You wanna talk to your girlfriend, right?" Before I can answer, he vanishes with his smoke rings.

❏

Karen picks up on the first ring. Her silky "Hello" is a Siren call.

"Hello, yourself. Before you say anything else, tell me what you're wearing. I want to visualize you just as you are."

"Okay," Karen replies. "I'm wearing a sort of tight-fitting sweater."

"Excuse me while I wipe my chin."

"With a cardigan over it."

"Okay."

"And some loose, slinky slacks."

"Yes, yes, I like. And?"

"And a pair of clunky white Adidas."

"You're in your nursing outfit?"

"However did you guess? Just walked in after a double shift; doubled up today because tomorrow we're leaving."

I can't bring myself to reply. By playing my waiting game, I've lost my chance to see Karen before she leaves.

"Ovid, are you still there?"

"Sure. Sorry. I'm disappointed you'll be gone, but I understand. It's just that I . . ."

She overrides my plaintive words. "I miss you, too, Ovid. But we'll see each other soon."

What I want most now, for some odd reason, is to kiss and taste Karen's tanned and freckled shoulder.

"Are you there, Ov? You seem so distant. What are you thinking about?"

"Your tanned and freckled shoulder."

"Ovid, weird Ovid, I think you need a great big hug. Wait a minute, April's dying to talk to you."

"Hi, Ovid, how you doin'? You owe me sixty two bucks. And I hope you don't mind, but I ran out of big words so I've been using two more Harper's."

"Good idea, kid. Keep reading, keep writing." I'm feeling magnanimous. "Is that sixty-two bucks figured at the full dollar rate?"

"Dollar rate? You said half-dollar."

"I just now said dollar. I doubled down. May do it again till you run out of words and blow the whole thing."

"Fat chance, Ovid." I can hear her built-in calculator multiplying her earnings by two.

"Well, don't throw your brainpan outta whack, kid. But I may have to ask your mom to cut off her Harper's subscription. How you doing with that photo I sent?"

"Ellie—that's my friend—'shopped it, but it's not too clear. She wants to keep trying."

"Good enough. Thanks, April. Please ask Ellie to send me what she's got early tomorrow. Put your mom on again."

Karen's back on.

"You've got my kid diving into Harper's *and* the dictionary every day now. She actually loves doing it. Look, I know it's late there, so I'm going to say goodnight. I wasn't going to take my phone on the trip, but I just decided I would. I'll only answer if it's you calling. Don't want you to get too lonely. And, just to let you know, I don't think our little separation is going to 'do us a lot of good.' If it was my choice, I'd have you here with us. In the Sierras. But right now April and I do need to be alone together. I know you understand that, Ovid."

"I do. Goodnight, Knight."

"Goodnight, my Ovid," she echoes. Then she adds a soft double-kiss.

The sound of the kiss reverberates in my head. I sleep the whole night without waking.

39.

Next morning, I check my email for the doctored photo. Nothing, just a message saying Ellie's still working on it because the faces are too small and too out-of-focus to enlarge well.

My hopes for learning what Thornhill looks like are about gone. I'd looked him up on Facebook but he wasn't there. I'll wait one more day till Ellie's best effort arrives.

So I have Nate drive me up to my Bernie's grave in Cleveland Heights. I sort of abandoned my father years ago—not that much unlike my mother did—to chase my career muse west. Whatever, I feel a compelling urge to touch the places I haven't seen in over twenty years. Mostly, to touch the place where he rests. To touch him.

❏

Cleveland Heights is an old East Side suburb atop a hill overlooking Cleveland proper. It had once been thickly populated with Jews who'd moved eastward from the city's center, with its numbered streets, in the typical river-flow pattern that brought the black population in its wake. In the past scores of years, most of Cleveland's Jews continued their eastward move to the farther suburbs of Beachwood, Pepper Pike, Chagrin Falls and beyond. The spread of the diaspora works in this river-flow fashion in most big American cities. Today, Cleveland Heights, as in the past, remains the most eclectically mixed of all Cleveland's sixty-plus suburbs.

Of its fifty thousand-plus residents, nearly half are black. The others are white and mixed race with many Asians and Indians. Many are professionals, among them academics, the medical community and members of the acclaimed Cleveland Orchestra (the world's best, don't argue with me). Just down the hill are Severance Music Hall, the Cleveland Museum of Art, a sprinkle of other museums, Case Western Reserve University, the noted Cleveland Clinic and other hospitals and institutions which comprise Cleveland's cultural, educational and health-care core known as "University Circle."

History lesson ended.

❑

"Var toe, Boss?" asks Nate for what seems the hundredth time.

I have him stop at my favorite bookstore, Mac's Backs, on Coventry, where I pick up a pristine hardcover of Spillane's "I, the Jury." Then, after lunch at the venerable Tommy's, I stop a few doors down at Diamond's flower shop for a dozen of the orange-yellow daffs my father once loved to plant by the dozens in our yard. After, I do a run-by of the many Cleveland Heights homes I lived in: the first little brick one on Shannon that my dad bought for under ten thou, the refurbished carriage house overlooking Little Italy, the mini-mansion I'd last lived in next door to Coventry Elementary in what was once a hippie neighborhood. Then, impulsively, I drop into the Coventry Library, just across from the school.

❑

The ivied brick building hasn't changed a bit in the half century since my mother first brought me there. That day changed my life dramatically. She introduced me to King Arthur and his Knights of the Round Table. One after another, I read every tale of his derring-do, then every fairy tale and juvenile sports story; six books a week till I exhausted the library's shelves. The place conjured the best, if rare, memories of my errant mother. Her presence here is palpable. My love of reading was my mother's faded—and only—positive legacy. What brought her to will it to me scant years before she walked out on the family?

The children's section miraculously holds many of the same books in the exact same place where I first found them. This simple fact of immutability staggers me. I close my eyes and see the little boy I'd been, sitting in my shorts and striped T-shirt and Boy Scout shoes, lying on my belly or sitting cross-legged at my mother's feet, as transported by my books then as I am in their recall now.

My mother, in a wicker chair next to me, so young herself, so beautiful, is daydreaming her way through Variety and some movie magazines, waiting for me to select the books I'd read in the next week. I detect her special scent mingled with the musty smell of the old books, a redolence that hovers still over my daily work.

I half expect to see her when I open my eyes. But she isn't there, nor is the little boy. I'm overwhelmed by what my mind's eye has shown me. Shaken by these incredibly vivid images, tears welling in my eyes, I half run toward the exit.

"May I help you, sir?" asks the librarian, an alarmed look on her face.

"No, thank you," I reply, composing myself. "Just visiting a few old memories. A few old friends."

40.

A few old memories, a few friends.

A powerful nostalgia.

It's time for Lake View, the cemetery that begins in Cleveland Heights and flows down a hill carpeted with daffodils and irises, rhododendrons and azaleas, pines and weeping willows and stately Japanese maples.

To this day, I've never witnessed a more serene and beautiful spot. It's the resting place of President James A. Garfield, John D. Rockefeller and most of Cleveland's founding fathers. At the north edge of a small tranquil lagoon, in the shadow of the simple but elegant Jepthah Wade Chapel with its exquisite stained glass Tiffany window, in a small plot marked by a simple block of granite that rises just inches above the ground, also rests Bernard Kent, né Kornfeld.

There's no one in the vicinity. This is the way I liked it when I came here growing up. The solitude allows me to better feel what I'm feeling for my father. God, I miss my old man. But I guess I didn't miss him enough to stick around.

I often biked in with friends, sometimes girlfriends, to eat picnic lunches at the lagoon's edge and feed the leftovers to the ducks. Before my father ever mentioned the matter, I felt, as a boy, that our entire family, not requiring a "Jewish" cemetery, should someday be buried here in this non-sectarian one. I later convinced him to agree upon the lagoon location and to buy a small plot next to it for me . . . "just in case." He said he might buy it for Clotilde . . . "just in case." The idea became an ugly joke to me. But he bought the plot anyhow.

I kneel at the grave near which a Japanese maple grows, planted by me after his funeral. I brush away the leaves from beneath the maple and wipe the dust and grime from my father's small headstone. Then I use the tissue wrap from my flowers to make a pencil rubbing of the stone's inscription as a keepsake. And a reminder to visit him again. When the rubbing is complete, I fold it carefully and pocket it, then set the daffs gently on the mounded dirt and, while still kneeling over the grave, recite the opening words, the only ones I remember from the *Kaddish,* the blessing for the dead. *Yisgadal, v'yiskadash shmei rabah . . .* I repeat these ancient words three times to atone for my ignorance at not knowing the rest of this most sacred of Hebrew prayers. Then, as I pass my hand over them, I read and reread, aloud, the words he wanted carved into his stone.

Bernard Kent
1919-1984
Beloved Husband, Loving Father

Beloved husband? Beloved by whom? By me, his son, absolutely, but hardly by my mother. It was like my father to insist that his inscription be kept to a few pedestrian words. He wasn't big with words. It was also like him to insist that the woman who'd been unfaithful to him, and had run off and left him and his young son, be forgiven and remembered with such an outrageously false word as "beloved." He was a remarkable man, a good man. And a weak man.

Along with the sorrow of recalling my father's death, an anger is welling in me. It often arises when I think about my mother. Bernie Kent deserved to live longer than his sixty-five years, and would have, I'm certain, if he'd lived happier; if he hadn't chosen to remain alone. And he deserved much better than what he got from his Clotilde. I deserved better from her, too. You got me to love reading, mother dear, but, goddammit, woman, you sure as hell gave me no reason to love you for anything more.

I resent the intrusion the recollection of my mother is making on the gentle memory of my dad. But I'm troubled as much by seeing myself as having abandoned him too. What else can you call my leaving town a few years before he died? I left him a lonely and broken man. I had his blessings, of course—it was like my dad to bestow them—but I'm sure his loneliness, due to my leaving, hastened his quick decline and death. I don't want to think about it anymore. Not in this quiet and peaceful moment. Not in this perfect place.

But I can think of nothing else. My tears begin to flow. I lie prostrate, put my arms around the headstone and rest my head heavily upon it. I beat the yellowing grass over Bernie's grave. "Damn you!" I shout. Who am I damning? My father? My mother? Myself? All of us?

41.

I'm lying there a few minutes, spent, not moving. Suddenly, an eerie feeling of being watched comes over me. I jerk my head up in time to glimpse a black-clad figure disappear behind one of the fluted Doric pillars of Wade Chapel across the small lagoon. Whoever he is, I'm now certain he's been watching me all this time. Who the hell has the nerve to do such a thing? Who would know I'm here unless they followed me? Is Thornhill on to me? Is it his henchman, Harmony? Have they discovered me before I discovered them?

I jump to my feet and break into a run around the lagoon to the chapel. A limousine and a liveried chauffeur are parked in the chapel's U-shaped drive, but the chauffeur is alone, leaning against the driver's door and smoking a cigarette, obviously waiting for his passenger who is likely in the chapel. Or spying on me.

Before I can reach the chapel's heavy wooden doors, I again see a slip of black flap from behind the same pillar. I march toward it, my anger boiling over.

"Whoever the hell you are," I splutter, "if you'd like to continue your goddamn spying, come out and do it close up. Come out so I can see you, you bastard!"

No response. Just the eloquent silence of the cemetery. Then, slowly, a painfully thin old woman emerges from the pillar's shadow. She's dressed smartly in a black raincoat over a black suit with a long skirt. Supported by a Malacca cane, she appears to be in her eighties. She stands, straight as a maple sapling, as if she's making a stage appearance. She does not seem to be affected by my challenge. For some time, without speaking, she stares at me, both hands on the cane before her.

I return the stare, fascinated, unable to take my eyes off her. I haven't seen her in nearly forty years, but I recognize her just as surely as I recognized the Babe. The cold, black eyes and the firm set of her mouth are unmistakable.

"Clotilde?"

This is less a question than an accusation.

"Ovid," she acknowledges, evenly. Her tone suggests no apology for her rude intrusion. Though she'd seen me and must have known what was going through my mind at my father's grave, no attitude of concern appears on her surprisingly un-lined face. Nothing has changed. Cold, cold Clotilde.

I can't speak the thoughts exploding in my mind. Curiosity is arguing with my rage, but the utter shock of seeing my mother, after all these years, is short-circuiting my tongue.

"Why are you here, Clotilde?" That's all I can think to ask.

She seems more ready to confront me than I am to confront her. She takes her time answering. "You've gained a lot of weight, Ovid."

Oh, great. A classic Clotilde. Is that some kind of a joke? Hasn't seen me in all these years and all she can say is . . .

"Ovid, my son," she goes on, "are you really interested in why I am here?" Before I can reply, she asks another question. "Would you rather ask questions than answer them?"

Interesting question in itself. Her voice, if thinner, is still dramatic, her diction as perfect as her carriage. She remains ever the actress/dancer. I forget her crass first remark. Yes, I have a few questions to ask my beloved long-lost mother. A few dozen. But, in my confusion, it takes me a minute to answer the two she's just asked.

"Yes, Clotilde." That's how she always preferred I refer to her. She thought it was sophisticated. "I would like to know why you're here. And I have questions I haven't even thought of yet. But first I have to get used to the fact that you *are* here, that you're actually standing in front of me, that you're actually still alive, because how could I possibly know?"

Not replying, she begins to waver. Have my comments thrown her? I hope so. She's doing her best to show her strength, but suddenly she seems ready to collapse, likely from the equal shock of seeing her son so unexpectedly. She takes one hand off her cane and grasps for the pillar. Her eyes become glassy. I involuntarily move toward her. She falls into me, dropping her cane and throwing her arms around me in a desperate attempt to remain upright. Is she acting? *Still* acting?

I'm not ready for the electric shock of this physical contact. She feels like a sack of bones. Though tall—she might yet be five-eight—there's no substance to her. She can't be ten pounds over a hundred.

Is she reacting to our first touch since I was little? Would I walk with her around the lagoon, she pleads. I grind my teeth and look up at an ominously overcast November sky. Okay, all right, I will. Will I please hold her arm? Yes, why not? Whose doing is this? My father's? Is he watching this sad scene? Directing it?

If the Babe—or his Boss—has anything to do with this I'll never forgive either of them.

For fully five minutes we say nothing. The sun takes its cue to look in, flinging shards of light at us from behind a stack of nimbus clouds, accentuating the fading reds and yellows, the golds and greens of the leaves surrounding the placid lagoon. A fall chill is in the air. Clotilde speaks first. "If you're wondering what I'm thinking Ovid, it's what you would most want to know. I suppose most of your questions would begin with *why*."

"It's a little late for why questions, Clotilde. But I am curious why you're here. It's not a coincidence, is it?"

"Here in Cleveland, or here at the cemetery today?"

"Both, I guess."

"It's only somewhat of a coincidence. I moved back to Cleveland from New York six years ago, shortly after my husband, David Lazarus, passed on. I've come here to the cemetery every year since for the anniversary of your father's death, his *yahrzeit*." The word sounds strange coming from her. She was born to liberal parents whose Jewishness was far less important than their socialist politics. Though raised as a Jew, she always seemed to avoid any appearance of being one, never even using the Yiddishisms that everyone in her crowd used. Surprising then that her second husband would also be a Jew, like the first.

She continues. "I felt strongly, from the day I returned, that I would see you here someday, that you, too, would return on an anniversary day. You were always rather sentimental that way."

How can this woman presume to know her son so well? She goes on: "That possibility of your returning, even more than the memory of your father, is why I come here." This is a lot for her to admit. Then, without blinking, "Have you come back to stay?"

"No, Mother, I'm leaving in a few days for San Francisco. I've lived there for years. I doubt if you knew that."

Her crooked smile tells me that she does know that. It tells me, too, that she's been waiting for me to call her "Mother." A typical Clotilde contradiction.

"You say you're curious about why I returned," she says. I nod. "Do you also care to know what has happened to me in the years since I left you?"

"No, Clotilde, I do not. And you didn't leave us, you abandoned us." I have to control my anger because I'm not just talking to my mother; this is a frail old woman, of limb, if not of mind. That's my mother all over. Still, I'm not going to waste this opportunity to say my piece.

"Mother, more than anything else, I would like to know how you could disappear and never speak to us again, never let us know where to find you, never even try to contact us. I don't know exactly what you had against"—I'm about to say "my dad"—"against the man you dumped. I need at least to understand that part of it."

I'm helpless to stop, and not yet ready to hear her reply. "And why did you dump *me* like that? You walked out one day. Just like that. How can a mother do that to her child? I thought you loved me. How could you do that to *me*? Explain that. Explain that."

She stops walking. She's been looking straight ahead, her jaw set all the while my rage is building. But now, wavering again, she gestures toward a wooden bench at the water's edge. I guide her to it. We sit at opposite ends. Looking ahead, not at each other.

Resting a moment, she turns to me and speaks. "Your father was a very good man, Ovid. Though he didn't know how to show his love to me, I always knew he felt it. He couldn't show it much to you, either."

I stop her with two hands raised. "No, Clotilde, maybe he wasn't good at speaking his love, but he showed it to me in ways you didn't, in ways you'd never understand."

She sighs and waves my angry gesture off. "Listen to me, Ovid. As much as your father loved me, he never understood me, never accepted that I needed more than the life I was leading."

"And what was so wrong with 'the life you were leading?'"

"Oh, come now, Ovid, don't be naïve. I wasn't cut out to be a housewife, nor, admittedly, a mother. Which, in those days, was the only choice a woman had. My only way to express myself was to act and dance in amateur theater. You remember, I even brought you along to act in children's parts a few times. You're not aware of it but, though I was gone, I pulled strings to get you that job at the Hanna Theater after college."

"That hardly . . . Is there more of this, Clotilde?"

"David was the director for the South Pacific road company coming to Cleveland. He was here to audition local actors for a few small parts. Trying out is how I met him. He was charming, sophisticated about the world of dance and music and the stage, about the world in general. I liked to think we spoke the same language."

It's obvious she's remembering this "charming, sophisticated" David, not giving a damn about the plodding, workaday Bernie Kornfeld who gave up his family name in vain to make his Clotilde happy. But why is she telling me this?

"He didn't give me a part, but he took me on as a script girl. We somehow hit it off."

I do not need to hear this. I allow myself to nonetheless. She's old.

"I was still young and impressionable. David asked me to leave with him and, on a crazy whim, I did. He was for real. My life suddenly became exciting." She doesn't turn to see if I'm still listening.

"Does this story have an ending?"

She continues as if she hasn't heard me. "When he asked me to marry him, I asked your father for a divorce. It was the only thing, the last thing I ever asked of him. He gave it to me without saying a word. Who knows, if he'd fought for me . . ."

"I finish her sentence: ". . . you'd still have left him. But he couldn't say a word even when the sky was falling."

She still doesn't seem to hear me.

"He—David—was a good man, too. But he never loved me as deeply as he loved his work, as deeply as your father did, this I knew. Years later, David was stricken with pancreatic cancer. It was a difficult time. I don't know what came over me when he died. Perhaps it was my finally recognizing the depth of your father's unequivocal love. Though Bernard was gone, I wanted to spend the rest of my years here with him, not in New York. I had nothing here other than Bernard's memory, other than this place where he was. But that came to matter more than what I had left in New York. That's all that mattered. That, and you.

Though I knew where you lived, I could never bring myself to tell you that."

She stops, pulls herself together, then continues.

"I flew here every year on this date, and finally just moved back here. It's not much of a gesture and it's not really meant to be an apology, but it's my only way of making up for what I did to him. I'm here at the cemetery not just once a year, Ovid, I'm here every month, sometimes more, if that means anything to you. I'll tell you this, it means a great deal to me because it puts me as much at peace as I've ever been or expect to be. That's what I doubt you understand."

❏

I think about her last statement. "Clotilde, you've told me how you felt about my father and this . . . David person. You say you finally understood how deeply my father loved you. That may be true, but that makes it even harder to understand how you ever could have left him. That's all I have to say about that. Now, would you mind telling me how you felt about leaving me? Did you understand the depth of *my* love for you? How did it feel to abandon your only child?"

My anger is making me over-enunciate my words. I immediately regret what I'd just said. But I feel relieved, too, to get it off my chest.

Clotilde says nothing. She remains sitting stiffly upright. Her gnarled hands are affixed to the handle of that Malacca cane. She stares in the direction of her first husband's grave across the wind-rippled lagoon.

Finally: "Though you may not choose to accept my explanation, Ovid, I fully understand your anger. But will you hear what I have always felt about my—you named it for what it was—my abandonment of you? The truth is, I don't understand it myself and likely never will. I didn't know what was right. Or didn't want to know. I was still immature. I knew you wouldn't accept what I did, therefore you'd never accept or forgive me. But, having done it, I thought I'd be doing both of you a favor not to fight for your custody."

"You never wanted my custody."

Clotilde sucks in her lips before speaking. "Okay, you needn't rub it in. I did not deserve you. Never did." She pauses and sinks into herself. She's shrinking before my eyes.

She begins crying. Something I've never seen her do except on the stage. Is this an act, too? I'm leaning forward. My hands are locked between my knees. I'm looking up, out, anywhere but directly at her. I'm ready to explode.

Neither of us speak for a full minute.

Then she stops crying and sits upright again. "I felt horribly guilty about you, Ovid, as soon as I left. I'm certain that comes as no surprise. I *was* guilty, I'm *still* guilty. I couldn't bring myself to phone or write because I had no words to explain myself. As time passed, I kept putting that impossible task out of mind. I didn't know what to say then and I'm afraid that I have no explanation now. I prayed you'd just figure it out for yourself some day and forgive me. Or, at least, not hate me."

I'm still not looking at my mother. "What did you know about praying?" I say. "I didn't know much either, I was never taught how, but I prayed you'd stay." Now I turn to her. "Look, Clotilde, did you ever think of saying you were sorry? I mean, back then, did you ever think of saying those two simple words? Have you ever once, since then, thought of saying them? Just plain 'I am sorry?'"

"Yes, yes, yes, that's all I thought of. I wanted to say that a thousand times. But I couldn't find a way to say it even once. I *was* sorry, though. I *am* sorry. I am so very, *very* sorry." She pulls a dainty linen kerchief from her cuff, brings it to her face, blows her nose and keeps it in front of her face as she begins to sob again.

From where the feeling arises I don't know, but I'm tempted to put my arms around her. I fight the urge successfully. Now I, too, look across the lagoon at the grave. I can see it clearly in another shard of sunlight. So clearly that I see a crusty leaf fall upon Bernie's stone. Nature honoring my dad. Nice touch, Nature.

"Mother . . ."—the word slips out again—"there's something I need to tell you. You apparently haven't thought to ask what's become of my life, but I'm going to tell you anyhow. Like any guy, I met a lot of women. Most of them the wrong ones, a few, the right ones. I never got married though. Nothing lasted even more than a few months. I suspect you can figure out why. Anybody might if they knew my story. But it took me years to finally get it. *I did not trust women.* That simple. Every time I got close to one, I ran. You know why I ran, Clotilde?"

She tries to wave off my next words. She's sobbing uncontrollably now. But, just as she can't stop herself from crying, I can't stop myself from saying what I need to say.

"You know why I ran, Clotilde? I ran because I knew that sooner or later *they* would run. Just like you ran, Mother dear. So I beat them to it, that simple. I didn't trust women because, just like Clotilde taught me to read, she taught me to *dis*trust women, *all* women."

She suddenly stops crying, sits up, turns to me, looks straight into my eyes, sets her jaw and slaps me across my face with all the strength her wizened arm can muster.

I hear the slap more than feel it. It stuns me into silence. But I'm more stunned over what I've just allowed myself to say, to reveal.

Clotilde is livid. Before I can ask why, and without apology, she tells me.

"Ovid, you may think you have the right to say anything you damn well please to your errant mother, your rotten mother, but you only know what I put you and your father through, that's all you seem able to think about. I'm trying to tell you what *I've* been through and you just will . . . not . . . listen. You never were much of a listener. You have no idea, none, what I've put myself through every day I've been away from you. You cannot have hated me more than I've hated myself. *Especially* for what I did to you. She stops and wills herself to rise, brushing off the offer of my arm.

I get a flash of Karen's anguished face as she was telling me how horrible she felt not fighting for April when she left Las Vegas. Is all this connected? Babe? God? Clotilde? What are you three doing to me?

My mother's voice fades in. "Ovid, you have never walked in my shoes. I sincerely hope you never do anything as sorry as I did to put you in them. But, until you have, just as you cannot or will not listen *to* me, I will listen no longer to your judgment of me. It's sanctimonious, that's what it is, and I won't put up with it, do . . . you . . . hear me? Now, either accept me for what I am or just plain shut up and leave me alone."

What? I have no reply. It doesn't matter, though. Shaking like the last of these November leaves, she's hardly finished talking.

"I don't need you to make me feel worse than I already do, my son, and I'll tell you something else. As much as I want your understanding and forgiveness, I damn well don't need either. I've lived without them for all these years, I'll die without them, too."

Silence. All I hear is the wind. I'm not ready for this. It hadn't occurred to me that my mother has given *any* thought to me after leaving. I was certain she hadn't. Was I wrong? In the state she's just put me, I have no ready answers. But after the silence she seems more collected.

"Ovid, my Ovid, have you any idea what I'm talking about?" she says, raising a hand to grasp my shoulder.

"I hear you, Mother," is all I can say. Then, pausing, I add, "I'll have to think about it."

"Good," she replies. "And while you do, I have a more difficult question. A request, actually. Something I've been thinking about for a long time." She drops her hand and stands up tall, both hands on her cane now. Still the drama queen.

I look at her, waiting. I know what she's about to ask.

"I want your permission to be buried beside your father, may I have it?"

I was right. Who is this outrageous woman? A pitiful, sobbing emotional wreck one moment, a ranting harridan the next. If I hesitate to answer, it's because I'm reeling from this latest shock, this unseemly, sacrilegious, absolutely unthinkable idea. I can't control a shudder.

"First, my dear mother, that does not sound like a question, it's more like a demand. And second, how dare you ask? How dare you even think of such a thing? Before you say another word to me, the answer is no. No, you may not be buried beside my father, beside the man whose name you stole before you left him. And if I have anything to say about it—and I do, legally even—I don't want you buried anywhere near him or anywhere in this cemetery. Go bury yourself beside your beloved David."

By now I'm hyperventilating. This last remark hits her like a well-swung fist, but I don't stop there. "You had my father so wrapped around your little finger. He loved you so much that, even now, if he could, he might be tempted to have you back in the way you have the chutzpah to suggest. But I don't think so, Clotilde, I do not think so. Even he would not be that much of a fool. And I, goddammit, I am not." As I speak, a drop of my rant-driven spittle hits her squarely on her heavily-rouged cheek. She doesn't even notice.

"Stop," she screams. She gathers herself to speak, but now, in a whimper, "Please stop, Ovid." Was this her primary purpose for being here? If so, it seems to have faded to nothing. The harridan has left her. She looks her years. Her voice has lost its sotto voce drama. "Let's just drop the subject, son."

Son? Hah! "Done," I say, my jaw muscles clenching and re-clenching.

We sit without talking, without looking at each other. I'm

wrapped in my own bitter thoughts. But my resolve is fading, too. I struggle with myself. Some craziness inside me is telling me to relent. Must be a trait I inherited from my father.

"Mother," I say. I say it slowly. "I hear your request. I'm sorry I attacked you like that, I am. I'm just not ready to think about allowing what you just asked of me. An hour ago I was thinking good things, things about my father. It was sad, but it made me feel good to be here, to remember him and talk to him. I knew why I was here. I understood it. Then you appear from nowhere with this impossible request. So I'm more than a little mixed up and not too sure of what I'm thinking or saying right now. I need some time to think it through. Is that okay with you?"

"Well, Ovid," she replies, composed enough now to repair her makeup from a compact she pulls from her purse, "I wish you'd think a little faster, because I'm not getting any younger."

A few beats pass till her remark registers. We turn to each other at the same time. Another beat and a smile grows on her face. Unable to help myself, I match it. We look at each other and start to laugh. To laugh. The release feels good.

And it feels bad.

But I'm not ready to forgive her. Or embrace her. Not hardly. Not now. Not yet. Maybe not ever.

"Mother, you are a piece of work," is all I can say. But the intended malice is missing in my voice.

We're both on empty.

❏

We resume our slow walk around the lagoon. Stopping again at the grave, I move toward the headstone to say my silent goodbye. When I return, my mother looks at me beseechingly. My eyes roll. I sigh, I shrug my shoulders. Then she makes her way, alone, to the grave. She motions to her chauffeur who has driven around to the roadway near the gravesite. He approaches and hands her a single red rose, a perfect red rose, which she drops on my daffodils. I get it right away. A ritual dropping of many single, perfect red roses. She stands, eyes closed, likely in communion with my father. She is tearless and ramrod straight again. The actress making her final exit. Then, saying nothing to one another, I walk her to the limo. As the chauffeur holds open her door, she fumbles around in her purse, pulls out a card and presses it into my hand. Only then does she allow me to help her enter. At no point does she seem to expect an embrace, nor does she offer one. All she says, through her open window, is, "Goodbye, Ovid." Her eyes are saying much more. Easy to read.

I instinctively reach for my card case, but leave my hand in my pocket. "Goodbye, Mother." These are my last words as the window closes and the limo pulls away. I notice the TLC marking above its rear bumper. The rent-a-limo makes it clear how important these cemetery visits are to her. Has she ever made a friend here?

Calmer now, I look at the gash her stark red rose makes across my pale daffodils.

Will I ever see or speak to my mother again? Will I grant her wish to lie next to her husband? Whadaya think, Bernie, should I let her in? I leave with the feeling that my father will find a way to answer me. Because, at the moment, I have no answer of my own.

Bernie Kornfeld was a man of few words, but he was never one to ignore a question from his son.

42.

Back in my room, I only want to collapse and unravel the meaning of this singular day. But I'm running out of time. I crank up my laptop. The Photoshopped ballpark photo has come through from Ellie at last.

Her message apologizes for its fuzziness and generally poor quality. Garbage in, garbage out. I can only guess which boy is the man I'm about to confront. He's probably pushed well past two hundred pounds because my guess is still Porky Pig, third from the left along the railing. Behind John and the Babe. I send my thanks and I.O.U. to April and Ellie.

It's nearing the dinner hour, preceding the cocktail hour, followed by the Thornhill hour. I take a slow shower, dress to impress, then head for the elevator.

Kind of wish I were carrying. A weapon also impresses. Then I remind myself how good I am with weapons.

The Bar is nearly empty. Chip nods a greeting and pours my drink as the Bambino eases his bulk onto the stool next to me.

"Good to see you," I side-mouth. "Can you believe what just happened?" He shoots me a knowing smile. I know he was aware.

"Your mother thing will take care of itself, Ovid. My hunch. Hey, I got your little embarrassment problem worked out, kid. You know that thing that looks like a hearing aid but ain't? I've seen a lot of them around. I think it's called blue teeth. You got one?"

"Yeah, Babe, Bluetooth. From my inside pocket I pull out a linty Bluetooth and pop it into my ear.

"Now, see," says the Babe, "when you're talking to me, you still look like an idiot, but no different than all the other idiots who use 'em."

"So what do you really make of today, Mr. Ruth?"

"I try to stay out of your private business, Ovid. Make it a firm rule to do so, which I sometimes break. But, from what I gather, as bad as you've had it, your mom's had it harder yet. You've made out better in life than she has. You might try going a little easier on her?"

"Advice received." Changing direction, I say, "I've decided to make my move this evening, Babe. Head on. Right after dinner." I make my tone sound very firm.

"What happens if you don't get to him, if your plans don't work?"

"Don't want to think about that."

"You really planning to rough up the guy?

"May have to. He's probably with a guy named Harmony. Sounds like he's Thornhill's armor. Maybe his boyfriend. Anyhow, it depends on how things go. I'd like to think that rough is not my style anymore, Babe. Smooth befits me."

The Babe sneers.

I take a slug of my martini before changing the subject again. "Babe, I know you can't talk to anybody down here, anybody, I guess, but me. But can you get in touch with anybody up there?" I lift my thumb unconsciously.

The Bambino leans in, interested. "Don't exactly know, kid. The Boss usually doesn't allow it. But if it means breaking a few rules, well, that never bothered me much. Who you got in mind?"

I explain that I want to reach my father. No conversation or anything, I say, just a simple question I need to ask him. Is that possible? The Babe says he isn't sure, he doesn't think the Boss will allow it. Not even for me. But he'll see what he can do. In fact, he seems kind of taken by the idea. Getting people together, for him, comes naturally and maybe a way of scoring a point with the Boss, and even of getting himself a notch up as a Proto.

So I lay my mom question on him.

He ponders it. "Good luck, tonight, Ovid," says the Babe, with one of his patented winks.

43.

Having had it with the swill at the hotel, I walk over to the New Yorker Deli on 12th, opposite the Southington. My martini buzz is a memory by the time I finish my matzoh ball soup and corned beef on rye. Damn, this town does rye bread a whole lot better than San Fran. None of that corn rye dreck. And they know how to slice the meat thin and still leave some fat on. Fat is the point of a good CB. Fat is a synonym for taste. Will someone please tell the rest of the world?

The Southington has changed a lot since I last saw it. Just like me, it's been around awhile and it's a little seedy. My hunch is that my quarry is up there now. So, I pray, is the montage. To make sure, as I approach the building, I punch Thornhill's pre-programmed number into my cell.

❏

A weak, high-pitched voice answers on the first ring. Nervous sort. "Hello?" The voice comes from someone who sounds like he wishes the caller hadn't called. I think he's IDed me but he doesn't know who I am.

"Harley Thornhill?"

He vamps a few seconds before replying. This is a man debating with himself about whether or not to lie.

"Yes?" His hesitation makes it sound like he isn't sure if he

195

is Harley Thornhill. If this is a professional thief, he's coming off as an amateur. Or not. Keep your guard up, Kent.

"This is Ovid Kent, Mr. Thornhill. I'm a private investigator from San Francisco." The P.I. reference suggests I'm packing. I wait for the information to sink in through the silence on the other end of the line. "Do you have any idea why I'm calling, sir?"

"No." He skips a few beats. "Well, yes, perhaps I do."

"In case you're not certain, Mr. Thornhill, allow me to fill you in. It's about what you've stolen from my client." I let that sink in, too. "My client has reason to believe that a montage with the autographs of Babe Ruth, Ty Cobb and Tris Speaker is in your—"

"How did you find me?" blurts Thornhill. There is discombobulation and fear in his quavery voice. The sound appeals to me. The fear can work for me. I've been on the right track all along. I have my man. Almost. I want to climb right through the phone and grab him by the throat and shake his—John Blackstone's—precious signatures right out of him.

Can it be this easy? "I'll answer your questions if you answer mine," I say. "May I see you? I can't tell you any more on the phone. I'm not here to trouble you any more than necessary, Mr. Thornhill. And I expect you to return the favor . . . and the montage immediately."

"But . . ."

"Am I making myself clear, Mr. Thornhill?"

Again, silence. "Yes, I understand what you're saying."

"And you'll cooperate?" I'm in my softly spoken, clear enunciation mode now.

"Yes, I guess I must," he says, sounding contrite and defeated. Then he adds, brightening up a little, "Of course I will. Are you in town? Where are you?"

"I'm downstairs at the Southington, Mr. Thornhill, walking through your lobby as we speak. I'd like you to buzz me in. Do you have a problem with that? You will if you say you do."

"Why no, Mr. . . . what did you say your name was? You're downstairs? Here in Cleveland?"

"Kent, Mr. Thornhill. Ovid Kent. I'm in Cleveland, I'm downstairs at the Southington, I'm coming up, got that?"

"Why yes, certainly, Mr. Kent. We can sit down and talk things over?"

"Why don't we, Mr. Thornhill? Repeat, I'm coming up." I hit the button next to 712 *H. Thornhill*. Through the phone I can hear my buzz in Thornhill's apartment.

"I'm letting you in now," he says. Nothing happens. An anxious half minute later I buzz again. Again, no answer. A stall? I hit the buzzer a third, fourth, fifth time. Finally the lobby door clicks open. I walk through and punch the elevator button. It takes what feels like an hour for the car to arrive. And ascend. As it does, I click my impatient nails against its wall till it finally crunches to a halt at the seventh floor.

❏

Suite 712 is at the end of a dimly lit hall whose once-thick-carpet is now worn thin. My long walk is slow and deliberate. As anxious as I am, I want to stretch this moment to its fullest. I knock firmly on the door and, from force of habit, step to one side while waiting for it to open.

The man who opens the door does not fit the voice on the phone. Must be Richard Harmony. He wears a black, tightly cut suit and a low cut, black silk T-shirt. His blond-tipped black hair, shorn at the side, is gelled to stand straight up from his square skull. He's maybe in his early forties, easily, six-three—with the hair, maybe six-four—and so broad I can't see past him into the apartment. He glares at me, offering no greeting, then stands aside to let me in.

A voice I recognize comes from the darkened, far end of the

duplex's living room. "Come in, Mr. Kent. I've been expecting the likes of you for weeks now. I guess I've been a bad boy. I imagine you'll be wanting to punish me somehow. Share a glass of wine with me and, afterward, we'll have our little chat."

This, I take it, is his real voice. The milquetoast cadence I'd heard earlier is gone, replaced, now, by a different, tone, a deeper, mocking one. I'm looking at Sidney Greenstreet in the Maltese Falcon. And I'm feeling like Bogey. But Sidney's sidekick is no wispy Peter Lorre.

"If you don't mind, sir, I'll skip the wine." I can hardly see the man, encased in deep shadows. The silent man one in black looks menacing. I overrule my earlier assessment of the task at hand. Not going to be easy.

"Mr. Thornhill, I hope you and your friend here won't give me a hard time about the autographs. Your attitude earlier suggested that you would not."

"Mr. Kent, surely you must surmise that a hard time would in fact be easy to give. Let's hope it's not necessary." Thornhill laughs heartily at his little joke. I don't. The man in black approximates a laugh but it comes out as a series of grunts.

"I have several questions. Mind answering them?"

"Not at all," replies Thornhill, rising and waddling into the light. He pretty much matches my hunch about his girth. He's about John Blackstone's age, short but distinguished-looking. He wears a pencil-thin mustache and has smoothed-back, yellowish-gray hair, probably a rug. Over his neatly creased gabardine trousers hangs a long silk dressing gown the likes of which I haven't seen since Noel Coward's "Private Lives." The man is, in fact, a parade balloon of Coward minus the cigarette holder. Which, to my amazement, he pulls out, loads and waits for a light from the widebody. Who wrote this script?

"Allow me," says Thornhill, "to introduce my companion, Richard." Harmony acknowledges the introduction with a scowl. "I'll not tell you his last name, because I don't wish to implicate him, although, by now perhaps, you know it. He's had nothing whatever to do with my acquiring the autographs."

Harmony not an accomplice? Thornhill has just marked himself for the liar he is.

"Allow me to stop you right here, sir," I say, playing my opening gambit by the book. "First, do you need to see my credentials?"

"No, Mr. Kent, I wouldn't trust them any more than I do your intentions."

I shift gears. "Then here's what I'd like you to know, Mr. Thornhill. I know that you did not commit this theft personally. But you and your friend, Mr. Harmony—of course I know his last name—can still go to prison as accomplices, charged with conspiracy to commit a crime and with receiving stolen property. Twenty year offenses, each." As if I knew. "It should, on the other hand, make you happy to know that my client is not anxious to prosecute either of you. Milton Blackstone just wants the return of the montage that has been stolen from his son."

Thornhill's head is nodding, I'm guessing not in agreement but to indicate that he hears me. I go on.

"If you don't return the montage, Mr. Blackstone will prosecute. It's that simple. He's a powerful, internationally known attorney himself. You wouldn't want to go up against him in any court of law. He'll have you arrested and file criminal charges, and he'll file a civil suit for damages, claiming, rightfully, and, I'm certain, successfully, treble damages for mental anguish, which indeed you have caused his son. And he'll sue for the return by replevin of what you now illegally possess. What I'm saying is that, fail to cooperate and he'll come down on you with both feet. Very heavy feet.

"But the fact is, Mr. Thornhill, he only wants what belongs to his son. Hand it over, here and now, you'll never hear from him or me again. I hope I make his and my intentions crystal clear."

"How did you know I was involved?"

"That's not for you to know. All you need know is that I have irrefutable proof that you were involved. Now *and* all those years ago at the Hollenden Hotel."

Thornhill's eyes bug out at my mention of the old Hollenden. "Very clever of you, Mr. Kent. But all of that notwithstanding, I see things in a rather different light. As you've learned—and admitted—I did not steal the autographs. What I did—*all* I did —was to purchase the montage in, I believe, a perfectly legal fashion. In doing so, I simply retrieved what was rightfully mine all along." Thornhill's eyes cloud over as he completes his statement. He stops and appears to be back at the Hollenden incident. "The signatures would have been mine all along had I played my cards right that day; had I not run out when I first saw Mr. Ruth and Mr. Cobb and Mr. Speaker."

He sounds a lot like John Blackstone. Bingo, Dr. Diavalone! And thank you, Dr. Ruth. The man fits their profile like a wet T-shirt.

Snapping back to the present, Thornhill continues. "Before you question me further, Mr. Kent, allow me to explain what has happened. When I am finished, you may ask anything you'd like. You may also find that I am fully justified in the legal purchase I made."

I'm not convinced by Thornhill's seemingly cooperative attitude. But the hulking Richard is mesmerized by the smooth tone of the voice behind it.

"That's fine Mr. Thornhill. I'm all ears and I've got all night." Although, truth tell, I'd like to be on the redeye returning to San Francisco—with the montage— by midnight.

But Thornhill needs to further justify his actions. Or maybe just talk. His explanation of what happened years earlier jibes almost perfectly with John Blackstone's; the extended scene in the Hollenden Cafe, the brief meeting of the two boys, the transferring of the baseball tickets. He even tells of hearing the story on WCPN, the Cleveland NPR outlet. And as he's speaking I spot the NPR anthology leaning on a shelf behind him. The man seems obsessed, in the truest sense, with the central fact that came galloping out of his mind that day: he must own, he truly deserves to own, *he does own* the unique, possibly one-of-a-kind set of autographs that have *wrongly* been held all these years by John Blackstone. His premise has become his fact. His lie has become his truth.

Hulk Richard sits there like a lump.

I sense a different scenario spiking through Thornhill's glibly gratuitous confessional. His body language tells me he's playing some sort of a game . . . and is about to show his hand.

"Mr. Thornhill," I say, after a longer period of silence than I'm usually capable of holding, "what exactly happened in San Francisco after you arrived?"

"Mr. Kent, you must believe that I didn't steal the montage. You do, don't you?

"I'm beginning to," Nothing to lose by this little fib.

"I simply purchased the signatures, the montage, for five thousand dollars cash."

"From?"

"Thomas, of course. Cecil Thomas. You must have expected as much."

Thornhill is, of course, correct. I not only have expected as much, I nod in agreement.

"Don't expect me to show you a receipt, Mr. Kent," he says, smiling. Harmony dutifully snorts out another laugh.

"Can you say more, Mr. Thornhill." I don't mind being this man's confessor.

Thornhill seems happy to say more. "I had written to John Blackstone earlier to make the offer. But I never heard from him. All I got was a late night call from Thomas saying that Blackstone was content with my offer but didn't care to deal with me personally, and that he, Thomas, was authorized by Blackstone to negotiate the sale, but the exchange had to be made in person, had to go from his hands into mine directly. Blackstone would not be involved, he wouldn't explain why. Frankly, I doubt

Blackstone ever saw my letter, my legitimate offer. If he had, I doubt he'd have considered the sale at any price. Nor would I had our positions been reversed, but I had to give it a try."

And *I* doubt that I'll ever see a copy of Thornhill's letter, if indeed it had been written. He's not the self-incriminating kind.

"May I see a copy of your letter, sir?"

"I didn't make a copy. Incidentally," says Thornhill, "I was prepared to offer twice as much had Thomas insisted, but, oddly, he accepted my first terms at once."

Finally, a statement with the ring of truth to it. Something is indeed odd here. Thomas is obviously intelligent enough to realize he could have milked Thornhill for more. Could he have some other purpose in mind than making a nice chunk of quick cash? Something else to think about.

"Anyhow, Richard and I flew to San Francisco, met with Ruggles at a bar he favors, paid him the money in hundred dollar bills and left a few days later with not just the autographs, but the entire montage, which—I can't say why—the man insisted we take. Perhaps he wanted to make its departure look like a casual theft, I wouldn't know. You, see, Mr. Kent, I'm doing your work for you. Any more questions?"

"Just two. Were you aware of—or responsible for—any break-in at the Blackstone residence?"

"No, absolutely not. I've just told you we were never anywhere near the home. I had no cause to go there once I had the signatures." I accept this. I have a copy of his E-ticket. "You said there were two questions, Mr. Kent?"

"Yes. May I have the montage now?"

Thornhill gazes at me for a moment, then breaks into a good imitation of Greenstreet's laugh. "You actually expect me to hand over what I have legally purchased? Please don't take me for a fool, sir. This meeting is over." Harmony stands up and hovers over me to assure that what his beloved says is so.

"This meeting is most definitely not over, Thornhill," I say, dropping the mister and any further pretense of cordiality.

"What I take you for, 'sir,' is a thief and a liar. A thief because you accepted goods you knew were stolen, a liar because you haven't stopped lying since. But though I'm not sure who's the bigger thief here, I am absolutely sure your so-called purchase will not stand up in court. No, you're no fool, Thornhill. You know as clearly as I that Cecil Thomas stole the montage, that it was not his to sell. So hand it over and we'll call it a day. If not, you'll have the Blackstones and the law to answer to. And me. Here and now." I hear myself making this dramatically hollow threat but I don't fully believe myself. Bogie would have said it with more conviction.

Thornhill puts on a properly cowed face. He's already proven himself to be a pretty good actor. Harmony is looking like a pit bull on a chain leash. Is that actually a blackjack hanging from his hip pocket? "You're certain that, if I comply," says Thornhill, "no charges will be filed?"

"I'm certain. You'll just have to trust me. Give me that montage and I'm out of here. Gone. Bye-bye, ciao and arrividerci."

"You know, don't you, Mr. Kent, that the autographs should have been mine? It's only a quirk of fate that it wasn't me who got them in the first place."

"We've tilled that soil already, Thornhill. The autographs, please?" My eye catches the four screw holes in the wall next to Thornhill's desk. Judging by the small piles of plaster dust on the floor beneath the holes, I surmise that the montage was permanently affixed there just before I called, then was hastily removed as I was being stalled in the lobby. If Thornhill meant to return the sigs, they would still be on the wall or lying out in the open. The man is hiding them. *And* hiding the truth. Liar, liar.

Thornhill continues to gaze at me as if still deciding what he'll do. Then he sighs dramatically, bends down with some difficulty and reach into the desk's lower file drawer. Is a gun coming out? He's only supposed to be a demented autograph collector. I've dealt with plenty of them. I'm not too crazy about guns. What's Thornhill up to? And when will he unleash Harmony?

No gun. Instead, he brings to his desktop a roughly two-foot-long leather tube, a good six inches in diameter. He cradles it as one would a newborn infant. For my benefit or his pleasure? Slowly, he twists off the lid and removes the tube's contents, all the while staring straight at me. It's the Blackstone montage, obviously frameless now, hastily rolled, its cardboard mat now coarsely creased, but, clearly, still intact. He unrolls it and, with fitting pomp, holds it up and gazes at it lovingly. Looking at the back of it, I can see, by the light coming through the montage openings, that it's authentic. Or seems to be authentic. Something about it bothers me.

Thornhill obligingly turns the montage around so I can give it a cursory inspection. It all appears to be there: the photo of the Babe, the press photo of John with the Babe, and the kids behind them, including young Thornhill, in the background. I was right about the Porky Pig kid being him. I can see the boy in Thornhill's pasty face.

At the bottom is the sheet of sigs, the grail I seek, Babe's, big but neat scrawl in the middle, Cobb's in green and Speaker's small and off to the side. Then Thornhill snatches it away.

"Let's have it," I say, wearily.

For an answer, Thornhill, moving gracefully for a man who wears a size fifty-four belt,minimum, reaches into a side pocket of his dressing gown. With purposeful deliberation, he pulls out a silver cigarette lighter, lights it and directs its flame at the opening containing the autographs.

I make a motion to stop him, but am immediately grabbed from behind by the lumbering Harmony who puts a wrenching double nelson on me. As I'm being held, I watch the sheet of autographs poof into flames. It's gone in seconds, its charred edges the only reminder that it had resided in the opening for well over fifty years.

Harmony retains his painful hold as Thornhill grins diabolically and breaks into his demonic cackle again. "Forgive me, my dear Mr. Kent, but I have determined that, if I can't have this cherished memento of Mr. Ruth and his companions, no one shall have it." He sounds like a bad movie, the one I seem to have been in with him since I walked through his door. The cackle morphs into a maniacal giggle as he slides the montage, with its char-edged hole, across the desk to me.

"You wanted your montage, here it is. But I'm afraid your fee —and I'm certain it must be substantial—has just gone up in ashes." Bwa-ha-ha!

I am getting more than a little pissed off. With my baleful friend Richard distracted by Thornhill's snorfing of his pleasure, I snap both my heels squarely up into the thug's nethers. His next grunt is not one of pleasure as he releases his nelson to tend to his crushed cojones. Before he can fall I spin around, grab his lapels and snap his oversized head down as I'm snapping my own forward; something I did with substantial effect maybe a dozen times in my DEA career. The hollow thump resembles the sound of a watermelon tossed from an attic window onto a driveway. The butt doesn't do my concussion much good, but it's worth every ounce of additional pain.

Harmony, knocked cold, crumples like a spill of soiled laundry.

Turning toward Thornhill, caught in mid-cackle, I growl, "All right, you little bastard, no more games. Gimme the goddam autographs. Now!"

He looks more stunned than Richard Harmony before I put his lights out. "I can't, you fool. Can't you see they're gone?" As he stares at his fallen friend, a sweat of fear pops out on his smooth-shaven face. "I told you, Kent, if I can't have them, no-body—"

"Shut up, Thornhill," I interrupt. "The autograph page you burned was as phony as you are. It was a color photocopy you must have had handy just in case someone came knocking. It wasn't even a good copy."

"How did you know?" he whimpers.

"Just figured it out. No loose-leaf holes at the edge of the sheet. Just the *image* of holes. You made the mistake of letting me see the back of the montage. The opening covered up the holes from the front. Now," I demand, "give me the sigs—the real autographs—or I'll remove your precious Richard's ugly face." My fist is ready to flatten the goon's sharp hook of a nose. "Then I'll remove yours."

"I can't, possibly. I won't. They're mine," he whines.

Harmony's eyes open. I let my punch go. His eyes close again as a spurt of his blood paints an interesting Rorschach on Thornhill's lovely, white wall-to-wall. For my encore I reach back to my old playing days as a Cleveland Heights fullback to lay a forearm shiver to his temple. It dents my elbow almost as much as I hope it dents his thick skull.

Thornhill screams as though I'd dropped the blow on him. His precious Richard is unconscious once more. Never taking his beady eyes off me, the effete little man reaches into the back of the desk's left-hand drawer. This time, still smarting from the shiver while nursing my head butt headache, I'm not paying close enough attention. What he pulls out is not the original loose-leaf sheet, but one of those old-timey police .38 revolvers which he quickly, if shakily, points at my forehead.

This autograph collector wants to play rough.

I make a quick decision. I can acquiesce to the higher power that Thornhill now possesses, or I can do something else. Aided by an adrenaline rush and my judgment of his sixty-something reflexes, I choose the something else.

Without hesitation I slap the revolver out of his hand. Never taking my eyes off him, I snatch it up from the rug where it lands. Then I turn and deliberately aim it below Thornhill's ample belly while carefully squinting through its sights. Just kidding, I've already ruined a set of family jewels. I raise my aim and snap off two rounds, one past his left ear, the other past his right. I'm a pretty good shot at three feet. The sound fills the room. Ironically, one bullet rips into the NPR book that helped Thornhill find his precious sigs.

The squat man screams and cringes as a dark stain grows on the front of his immaculate gabardines.

I look away in disgust, then empty the revolver's magazine, dropping the bullets into one pocket, the impotent weapon into the other.

"Game over, Thornhill. The sigs. Now!

Still wimpering, he hesitates. I don't. I sweep his fancy desktop paraphernalia onto the rug, clamp my medium-large hand on top of his head and introduce his face to the top of his desk. "Ready for more?" I ask.

Groggy, simpering with tears now, he listlessly pulls out a brown, business-sized manila envelope and slides it across the desk's now-nosebloody surface.

I inspect its contents. The McCoy. I roll up the montage, place it back in the leather tube, stick the envelope with the sigs into my jacket's inside pocket, click off the recorder in my hip pocket and begin to walk out, my pockets filled and my mission achieved. Sort of.

Harley Thornhill, slumps in his chair, defeated. He puts his blood-begrimed face into his pudgy hands and continues to softly cry, much as he must have cried that long-ago day in the Hollenden. In this moment, the pathetic man looks more than ever like John Blackstone. I feel sorry for him. Until I think about John sobbing out his own broken heart.

"What about my five thousand dollars?" he whines.

"Forget about it.

"But that's not fair."

"Yeah, well life ain't." I never sounded like this during a DEA bust. Enough with the Bogey routine.

As I'm leaving, I stop beside the still-groggy Harmony, just now coming to. I re-aim my foot at the hulk's groin, but hold the pose. To hell with it. Then I walk out. But, before the door clicks shut, I'm reminded of the pain in my head, shoulders, elbow, fist. I walk back in, lift poor Richard to his full height, butt him into neverland again, and drop him like he's the other shoe. This is getting to be fun.

Fifteen minutes later I'm back at the Shelbourne, perched on my regular stool, throwing back Chip's frozen Gordon's.

"How'd you get those marks on your forehead, Mr, Kent?" asks Chip.

"Just keep pouring, kid, okay?"

❏

Before dropping into bed, I phone Leo and Eddie to fill them in and thank them. Leo wants to know if he should cuff Thomas. No, it's a private matter till it isn't, I tell him. I leave it at that.

"What're you going to do with him when you get home, Ov?"

"Damned if I know, Leo. Ta-ta."

44.

Next morning, Nate, generously rewarded, drops me off at Cleveland Hopkins. "Bye-bye, boss, you a good man. We make a good team. Holmes and Watson."

"Elementary, Nate. You're a damned good man yourself. Wouldn't have had a clue to finding my thief without you." I slip him my card. "You've probably got some cousins in San Francisco. Come out for a visit and who knows, maybe I'll make you a partner. We'll chase down bad guys and books together. I'll put you in charge of my Philosophy section."

"Don't kid me, boss, I might show up," he says. With this, and a wave of his hairy hand, Nasir Ibrahim Nissam slots his cab into the busy exiting traffic.

By noon, I'm flying westward over the Mississippi. What was it the old Cleveland Indians announcer, Ken Coleman, always said when he signed off his radiocasts?

"Roundin' third and headin' home."

❏

"Nice goin', Ovid."

The Babe settles himself next to my aisle seat just as the plane descends for its glide into SFO. "Gee, thanks, Babe," I say, as usual, out of the side of my mouth. "Don't forget to buckle up."

"Very funny, kid. But maybe some day soon I can do just that. Depends on how the Boss looks at my handling of your case. Hey, kid, maybe I'll see you back in San Fran.

And, with a swoosh, he disappears into the overheard vent.

Part III.

San Francisco

The bookseller observes his clients as they gaze, for the first time in a month, at the object they had sent him to retrieve; they are certain it had been lost forever. The moment is an emotional one. They express their joy and gratitude in warm words. But not everyone in the Blackstone household is happy. This story has not ended. The denouement is yet to come.

45.

I fling a hi to Ethel as I board my houseboat at four p.m. I've been gone for the better part of a week.

"Welcome home, travelin' man," she hollers back. "Servin' up a batch of burgers at seven. Wanna come by?

With Karen and April still away, and me too frazzled to deliver my precious package to the Blackstones immediately, I shout a grateful yes. Then I kick off my shoes and fall back onto my bed, my eyes staring at the ceiling and thinking about the loose ends I'll need to tie up before Karen returns. The warming afternoon sun is slicing through my bedroom window.

Exhausted, I fall asleep and don't move till seven p.m. when I'm given a beer can wakeup call.

"You comin' over?" comes Ethel's raspy shout, "or do I have to drink all these brews myself?"

I blink. It's nice to be home. And the burgers smell great. Better than they eat, as usual. Ethel and I finish off three beers apiece between her dirty jokes and my tales of adventure in the hinterlands of America.

Nice to be home.

❏

Reverse jet-lagged, I wake up a little after five the next morning and fix my coffee and bagel. It's way too early to contact the Blackstones, so I round up some bait and throw in a line.

I've already decided that, if I ever get lucky enough to snag old Doris twice, I'd throw her back again. My busted head notwithstanding, I owe the old girl a lot. Without her, I'd never have met Karen. Or the Babe. I wish Doris would show so I can properly thank her. No Doris, but I catch not one, but two lunker largemouths.

At nine, I call Milton Blackstone. Thomas answers in his officious manner. Is he aware of where I've been? I can't tell. Of course he is. He's aware of everything that goes on at Overlook. He brings the phone to the old gentleman.

I've been phoning in periodic progress reports, but have not yet revealed the successful outcome of my trip. Truth is, I've wanted to make the announcement in person to see the Blackstones' reactions. And Thomas's.

Particularly Thomas's.

Blackstone knows I'm due home. He knows everything right up to my climactic scene with Thornhill. "Welcome back, Mr. Kent. You are back, aren't you? I imagine you've had some harrowing experiences during your travels. Have you some good news for us?"

"I do, sir. I have the autographs."

"What?! You do? That's splendid, Ovid! That is indeed splendid." Now I'm suddenly Ovid to Milton. And I've never heard the old man so animated. "How soon can you be here?"

"Within the hour, Milton."

❏

Thomas, greeting me perfunctorily, looks more than a little green. He ushers me into the study where the Blackstones are waiting. Though he never looks at me, his face says he hasn't missed me.

"Welcome home, Ovid," says Milton, rolling up and offering his hand. "I trust your head is nearly healed?"

I nod. John, constantly rocking while staring at my briefcase, says nothing. I can't tell if his father has passed my brief report along or not. He raises a hand weakly to greet me, then folds both hands into his lap.

"Mr. Blackstone, John, I'm very pleased to see you both again. But, before I show you what I've brought, I must ask that Thomas remain in the room." I steal a glance at Thomas. I've never seen the man appear so uncomfortable.

"You will stay, won't you, Thomas?" commands Blackstone, giving me an odd look.

"Yes, sir," mumbles Thomas. He's standing now with his hands clasped behind his back, shifting from foot to foot like he needs to relieve himself.

To Blackstone Junior I say, "I have brought back your autographs, John." I've given myself permission to camp up the drama. "I've found your friends. Your Babe Ruth, Ty Cobb and Tris Speaker. I have brought them home to stay."

I'd discarded the ruined mat and the leather tube so I could travel light. I pull two envelopes from my briefcase and remove the contents of the larger—the photo of the Babe in uniform, the smaller photo of John and the Babe with Thornhill in the background, and the ticket stubs—and bring them over to John. He stops rocking, leaps up and clamps his hands together on his chest before grasping them.

He walks the envelope to the library table and lays each item upon it, adjusting each position so that each is spaced equally apart from and perfectly square to the other, as in the original montage. Blackstone has, by now, wheeled himself to his son's side.

Then John looks at his father for permission to open the glassine envelope. Milton gives him a thumbs up. Slowly and reverently, John removes the loose-leaf sheet, brings it close to his round-lensed, rimless glasses and inspects it for fully a minute, looking at its back and reverently running his fingers over its front as if he's never seen it before. A beatific look comes over him. The tears that follow tell us that he has confirmed their authenticity, fully recognizes his prodigal children and is deeply pleased by their return.

He holds the sheet of autographs to his heart before squaring it off with his other itinerant treasures. With great deliberation he turns to me and enfolds me in an awkward bear hug that expresses what he cannot say in words. I'm amazed at how much strength he has.

A broad smile comes to the elder Blackstone's craggy face, and with the smile, his own tears. Mine follow, I can't help it. Thomas's jaws are clamped shut. Finally, John monotones, "Thank you, Mr. Kent." Words he repeats three times while making a slight bow each time he says them.

Blackstone is too worked up to notice that his retainer, the frozen Thomas, a "member of the family," has expressed no joy whatsoever.

And now, Ovid," says Blackstone, "perhaps you'll tell us what transpired with you in Cleveland. But first," he adds, turning to his valet, "Won't you please, Thomas, bring us some coffee and refreshments? Come to think of it, forget the coffee, bring the Amontillado. The occasion calls for it."

Thomas turns, more quickly than is his fashion, to retreat in response to his master's request.

I hold up my hand. "Milton, please allow me to belay that order. I have something important to say to Thomas."

Blackstone, puzzled once more, shrugs his acquiescence and says, softly, "Thomas?" Cecil Ruggles Thomas looks ready to flee for his life. His back is now toward us.

"Please face us if you will, Thomas," say I.

Thomas slowly turns. His face has gone from green to white. Though at attention, he looks like a spinning coin about to topple. His unfocused eyes dare not look at us.

I give a purposely abbreviated version of my confrontation

with Harley Thornhill at the Southington. I hold back revealing the tale Thornhill told me. The details, I promise Blackstone, will be in a lengthy written report to follow.

When my narrative halts, Milton Blackstone sits quietly, the backs of his hands supporting his chin, contemplating all he's just heard. Finally, the old man speaks. "That, Ovid, is a most remarkable story. I must say, you've more than earned your fee."

"Well, Milton," I reply, "I thank you for those kind words. But I must inform you that there's more to tell."

46.

Blackstone sits straight up in his wheelchair. He must suspect what's happening. "Ovid, exactly where're you headed with all this drama?"

"There never was a break-in, sir. Nobody breeched your security the night of the theft. A theft did take place, but not in the way we've been led to believe. There was no one present in your home that night other than the three of you."

Blackstone's eyes narrow. Has he been in denial over what I'm about to tell him? "Are you suggesting this was—what?—an inside job? Speak, man." He's balancing now on the front of his wheelchair, like he wants to wring the answer out of me.

"Actually, sir, I'm not *suggesting* anything, I am making an accusation."

"It's got to do with Thomas, Right?" The old man's face has become as ashen as Thomas's.

"Yes, sir, I'm afraid it does," I say, as I watch the disassembling of the once implacable Thomas.

"Your Cecil Thomas stole John's montage, covering up the theft with a fabric of carefully concocted lies about a robbery. Then he sold John's montage to Harley Thornhill. For five thousand dollars."

❏

A noisy silence fills the room. Milton Blackstone slumps back into his wheelchair. When he finally speaks, his words are barely audible, and are stated without a trace of conviction. "That is preposterous, Mr. Kent."

So now it's back to Mr. Kent. Go ahead, Milton, shoot the messenger.

The old man, looking older than ever, turns to face his quivering butler. "Thomas?"

The word is a demand to confess, an accusation unwillingly made. Thomas maintains an odd posture. He has stood at an approximation of attention, but has shrunk a fraction of an inch with every word of my *j'accuse*. His normally immobile face now reflects a cornucopia of emotions. He may want to scream or cry, but what he cannot do is speak. He need not speak. His features, his posture, speak for him.

Blackstone turns to me and says, with an air of resignation, "Well, sir, let's have out with it. Let's hear the entire story. I don't want to just read it, I want to hear you tell it, every word of it."

I detail every word of Thornhill's story, of how he learned, through NPR, that it was John who had the autographs, then located John and wrote to him, or said he did, to make a purchase offer at almost any cost.

"This Thornhill actually offered to buy John's autographs?" Blackstone asks, obviously incredulous but calmer now.

"For five thousand dollars, yes. Ten thousand, if necessary."

"I cannot believe Thomas would commit such a heinous crime. And certainly not for such a paltry sum. We've been like family to him—and he to us—for nearly thirty years." He's now talking about Thomas, like John, as though he's deaf.

"You shouldn't believe it, sir, because I don't believe it either. It's not exactly true. Yes, Thomas did the deed. But not, I'm guessing, for such a 'paltry sum.'" Thomas looks like he wants to be in another country.

"Please make sense, Mr. Kent." The old boy doesn't want to believe a word I'm saying, but he sure as hell is listening.

"I believe Thomas had another reason for his actions." Blackstone's attention is locked on my words. "If, after your death, sir, your son were to pass on, what would become of his inheritance, of Overlook and all your holdings?"

The old man's face—normally red due to, I suppose, rosacea —turns crimson. Now he's ready to disembowel the messenger. "What has inheritance to do with this?"

"Please, sir, your answer," I say.

He stares at me, his lips tightly compressed, debating whether he'll reply. I stare back. He breaks: "John is my chief heir, obviously, Mr. Kent. On my passing, Thomas would receive a modest bequest. Only after John passes would Thomas inherit a substantial sum, a *rather* substantial sum. Most of the remainder, the bulk, goes to a charitable trust. Is that the answer you seek, sir?"

"Yes, Mr. Blackstone, precisely. Look, sir, this appears to be a case of burglary, hardly of anything else, I'm sure you'll agree. That's why I never thought to consider these questions earlier. But when John made his sincere if inept attempt at suicide, and it was later suggested to me by your friend, Laura Cunningham, that John's life could be in danger because of his remorse over his loss, the matter of inheritance did indeed begin to sift through my mind.

"The loss actually *could* have led to John's death, not his natural death in, say, twenty years, but his death here and now . . . a thought, I believe, that occurred to Thomas as well. What I began to ask myself is this: Could death be *made* to occur? Just as important, did Thomas believe that it could? And finally, if he did believe it, could this belief have driven him to commit this crime, not for the gain of five thousand dollars, but, ultimately, for many times that from his forestalled inheritance? The crime then becomes one not of mere theft, but of something far more serious. Attempted murder."

My pronouncement shrouds the still, silent air.

The full picture appears to be unfolding in the old man's still keen and analytical mind. "Go on, Mr. Kent." He's resigned himself to hear me fully out. Leaning back now and clamping his arthritic fingers on his wheelchair's arms, Blackstone is back in the courtroom listening to a key witness for the prosecution. But, in the process, he's fading.

"No one knew better how John would react to the loss of his beloved autographs. How it could actually kill him. Thomas, out for big game, concluded that he could accelerate that outcome when its scheme was presented to him by Thornhill. And it almost worked. No jury would call it murder, but I would and I do. Attempted murder. By greed."

Blackstone's mouth falls open. His courtroom persona, as I end my dramatic screed, has left him. A Parkinson's tremor shakes his hand violently. He brings it up to steady it against his chest. "How, sir, can you say such a thing?" But, as earlier, his words have no conviction.

Thomas is about to crumble. "I'm sorry, Mr. Blackstone. You brought me in just to retrieve the autographs. But I've felt compelled to bring you all my conclusions. Would you have it otherwise?"

He waves off my apology, which isn't really an apology. "The break-in, you say it never actually occurred?"

"Yes. I surmised—well, I suspected—as much when I found more glass beneath John's window than on the sill. That suggested that the window had been broken from the inside. That neither you nor John nor even your dog, Stinson, woke up when the alarm went off suggests that you were surreptitiously given Trazadone to keep you asleep."

Blackstone turns his attention to the quivering, still silent Thomas. "For God's sake, Thomas, sit down before you fall down." Thomas practically falls into the Queen Anne chair behind him, probably for the first time ever to sit in the presence of his astonished employer. His legs are splayed and his arms hang beside him, his dignity, dissolved.

I go on. "Thomas replied to Thornhill by phone. The trace of that call was how I located Thornhill. That phone call between Thornhill and Thomas brought Thornhill here where the montage was exchanged for the cash."

Blackstone nods his understanding. He doesn't bother to look at the evidence I submit. "I've heard enough, Ovid. But what made you think Thomas could harbor such a devious scheme?"

"Mr. Blackstone, I can't climb into your man's head. If you really want an answer, you'll have to ask it of Thomas. I'm not much at 'why' questions."

"Thomas?" says Blackstone.

The sagging Thomas, next to tears, attempts to straighten up before he utters a word. He has our rapt attention. He speaks in run-on sentences.

"Mr. Blackstone, I could never harm Mr. John or you . . . I never meant for this to happen . . . I knew John would not sell the autographs . . . I told the man that but he threatened to attain them by any means necessary. . . I feared he would come to Overlook and do harm to me, to John, to all of us, then . . ." He stops, puts his hands to his face and starts a keening cry.

Right here, right now, sucker that I may be, I half believe Cecil Thomas. He made a mistake. The biggest of his life. But I have never seen a human being so totally, so abjectly remorseful.

I allow myself to believe he's telling the truth about the threats. Thornhill, he with his revolver and his thug, Harmony, was capable of committing mayhem on the Blackstones. That's how much he wanted his goddamn sigs. But Blackstone appears unimpressed. "Then what, Thomas?" he says, rataplanning his fingers on the arm of his wheelchair.

Thomas continues his stream-of-consciousness confession. "The Blackstone longevity . . . it's a long time to wait, sir . . . it shouldn't have mattered, I know, I know, but something happened . . . inside me . . . I don't know what I was thinking . . . I'm sorry, Mr. Blackstone, I am truly, terribly sorry. He's suddenly sobbing, so hard that no further words can be understood. A trickle of mucus seeps from his nose. He doesn't seem to notice. I shake off a flashback to my mother's sobbing "truly sorry" speech at the cemetery.

Blackstone sits stiffly, his hands now in his lap. "You couldn't wait for John to die a natural death, is that it, Thomas?"

No answer from Thomas. His wailing fills the room. He slips out of his chair, falls onto his side and begins a rhythmic banging of his hands on the parquet floor.

The old man looks away in disgust, then sits in silence. By the set of his jaw, he's containing his agitation but not doing it well. He suddenly wheels himself to his desk, fishes a key from his vest pocket, unlocks a drawer and withdraws a thick pile of high denomination bills.

He then rolls himself toward the prostrate Thomas. "Leave me, you miserable, pitiful Judas. I will not prosecute you in a court of law. But hear me, Thomas, you will prosecute yourself for the rest of your despicable life. *And in my presence!*" With that, he flings the bills at his manservant. "There're the rest of your pieces of gold!"

For a second, the hundred dollar notes seem to hang suspended as if in a snow globe. Several settle gently on the servant's back. The man flinches as though hit by bricks. He starts to mumble something, an undecipherable curse or apology. Leaving the bills scattered about the floor, he literally crawls, then rises to slink out of the room, a dead man walking.

I sit there, blinking. What, I wonder, did Blackstone mean by *Leave me*? Was he dismissing Thomas permanently? Stranger still, what did he mean by being prosecuted *in my presence*?

Milton Blackstone is not exactly an open book.

47.

After I round up most of his Franklins, I ask Blackstone if he'd like a drink to calm himself. He's shaking—obviously not just from the Parkinson's—as he nods and motions me to the desk. He pours two stiff sherries for us. We drink them quickly and without speaking. The silence becomes awkward. I pour him another. Maybe a dozen of the hundred dollar bills remain on the floor. The effect is surreal.

"And now, sir," he says, acting as though the previous histrionics had never taken place, "I trust you've prepared a proper bill for my inspection?"

I hand him another envelope.

The old man adjusts his glasses, removes the statement from the envelope, lifts a hefty magnifying glass from the desk and pores over the numbers, his eyes just inches from the page. I picture him wearing a green eyeshade. Finding the bottom line, he nods his approval. "Fifty thousand dollars for services as requested and fulfilled. Five thousand, eight hundred and forty-two dollars and fifty-two cents for expenses. Fifty-five thousand, eight hundred and forty-two dollars and fifty-two cents, receipts attached. You like to be precise, do you not?"

I nod my yes.

"Worth it at the price, and then some, Ovid," he says, tossing the papers onto the desk as if they were a utility bill. "But, if I may, my autograph hunter,"—the humor in this sobriquet is encouraging—"I'd like to round up your total a bit, a bonus, so to speak." This said, he reaches into his center drawer, pulls out a large, Moroccan-bound checkbook, then writes out a check in his wobbly hand, rips it out and, with a theatrical flourish, presents it to me.

He needs my permission to "round up your total a bit?" He has it. I casually slip the check into my breast pocket without looking at it, without even patting it. I am, I convince myself, a class act.

"I thank you, Milton." I'm feeling so good I almost call him "Milt." It's been an inordinate pleasure to know both you and John, to have been a guest in your home and to have been in your hire."

"Aren't you going to look at it?" says Blackstone, his eye effecting a wink.

"I trust you, sir," I say, affecting a laugh. He offers a smile slightly tainted with disappointment. I'm tempted to look but I manage to maintain my super cool stance. I want this to be my private pleasure.

"Ovid," says Milton Blackstone, still looking a little miffed, "I'm certain I speak for John as well as myself in saying it's been a pleasure to have had you in our lives. You are welcome at Overlook any time. But now I must have a little chat with Thomas. I wish you the very best in all of your endeavors.

Are you sure you don't want me to remain awhile? Thomas might . . ."

"You needn't worry about me, Ovid. Now be off with you."

In a very nice way, I'm being dismissed. Without his father's bidding, John comes over to say goodbye. I put out my hand but, ignoring it, he gives me another huge hug. His voice is almost animated when he says to me, "I love you, Ovid." He pronounces it not "AH-vid" like everyone else, but "OH-vid." Sounds fine to me.

I choke out a weak, "I love you, too, John." In this moment,

I truly do. He is a sweet man. His reaction to the retrieved auto-graphs means almost as much to me as the check anxiously awaiting inspection in my pocket.

Then he plods off to his bedroom obviously to re-express his love to his great good friends, Mr. Ruth and Mr. Cobb and Mr. Speaker.

Milton Blackstone escorts me to the front door where we say our brief goodbyes. As I'm pulling out of the driveway, my rear view mirror reflects the man, now perched tall in his wheelchair, waving me out of sight.

❏

As soon as I pull around the corner, I take my eye off the road just long enough to pull out the check. *Seventy-five thousand dollars!*

The Cruiser jumps a curb and takes out a strip of Sea Cliff tree lawn that's smoother than a putting green. I stop, back up, jump out, pat down the strip, wave an embarrassed apology to anyone inside who may have been watching.

Thank you, Uncle Milty, I like the way you round up your numbers.

Driving directly to my bank, I look around. The Presidio, the Pacific, the Farallones, the Golden Gate, the Headlands, the burgeoning fog, none of them have ever looked so beautiful.

The End?

Hardly.

48.

Allow me to jump several months ahead.

Just last week, Blackstone invited me back. Said he missed me and there was something important, he wanted to tell me. When the fortress-like front door of Overlook opened, I was stunned to find Cecil Ruggles Thomas standing behind it, stiff-backed as ever, greeting me formally, but still unable to look me in the eye. Thomas? Still here?

Later, over his beloved Amontillado, Blackstone explained. "You're surprised to see our Thomas again?"

"To say the least, sir."

"You do recall, Ovid, that dark moment when you exposed Thomas?"

"How can I forget it?"

"And when I said to him, 'You will prosecute yourself for the rest of your life, and in my presence.'"

"Yes, I wondered what you meant. I still do."

"I meant simply that I would continue to retain Thomas so that I could witness his remorse for the rest of my life. It would be my most satisfying revenge."

I thought I knew Milton Blackstone. "That would seem almost as harsh on Thomas as dismissal, sir. But wouldn't that be almost as hard on you?"

"Well, some might feel that way. I did too, up to a point. But, as the Lord sayeth, 'Vengeance is mine.'"

I was surprised to hear a man known for his devout secularity quote this old saw. He recognized my reaction and laughed. "Actually, Ovid, it was simpler than that. I just didn't have it in me to follow through. And when it came right down to it, I was too used to Thomas to lose him. I didn't want to send him away, I, well, I just wanted to keep him around. But for the right reasons. What I'm saying is that I had a whole change of heart. So I devised what you might see as an unusual scheme. Interested?"

"I am, yes. Please go on."

He was grinning an extra-white grin. "I made Thomas an offer he couldn't refuse. I decided to scrap my old arrangement with him. Now, as soon as I die, he'll begin to receive an extra stipend, beyond his salary, of five thousand dollars for each month John remains alive and well. He will continue to be John's primary caretaker, and will be required to report weekly on his well-being to Laura Cunningham, who will oversee the special trust that provides the stipend. Then, after John passes, Thomas will receive a modest bequest."

I smiled a crooked smile. "If I read you correctly, sir, you'll be paying Thomas to keep John alive, not to, uh, expedite his demise."

"Precisely."

"I also observe that this allows Thomas an opportunity to cash in on your death, the sooner the better."

Blackstone almost fell out of his wheelchair laughing. I'm glad he was amused, not offended. "I'll take my chances on that," he told me. "Either way, he'll not have long to wait."

"But there's something I don't understand," I replied. "Your Thomas made it his purpose to shorten your son's life. How can you possibly trust him, under any set of circumstances, to oversee John when you're gone? How can you be certain, even with your generous 'stipend,' that he'll act as you expect and desire?"

"I can't be absolutely certain, Ovid. But at least he no longer has an incentive to do harm. Quite the opposite, I'd say.

"Frankly, sir, I'd have fired Thomas *and* filed criminal charges against him."

"Most would, I suppose. But I've spent a lifetime dealing with the criminal mind. Everything I've learned—everything I feel in these old bones—tells me that, with all the miserable humanity that *is* out there, Cecil Thomas is not a criminal; a petty thief, yes, but hardly a murderer. That was my epiphany. So I say to hell with what other people think!

"What about the five thousand he took from Thornhill?" I asked.

"Oh, that? I made him return it, of course. Look, Ovid, Thomas made a monstrously egregious mistake," he continued, "but one he deeply regrets. He is human, and, I believe, re-deemable, and I am taking it upon myself to give him that chance. In short, I have accepted Thomas's apology, and as far as I'm concerned, that is the end of the matter."

Milton Blackstone is also human. Eminently.

"Good summation, counselor. The prosecution withdraws all questions."

I marveled at the acuity of this amazing man's vital brain, brilliant right to the end.

❏

Milton Blackstone died just three weeks later. Of natural caus-es, if that need be added. And probably with that righteous grin still on his face.

At the funeral Laura Cunningham stood beside John. Cecil Thomas stood on John's other side. John didn't seem to under-stand that his father was gone. He still had his baseball games to amuse him. He did not cry. But tears flowed from those who stood beside him.

Milton Blackstone, *requiat in pacem*.

49.

Okay, I'm back. It's the day after I made my goodbyes at Overlook. I have three whole days with Karen after she and April return from their Sierras trip before she heads back to work. I'll make the most of them.

I'm happy. Ain't no other word for it.

And so is the Babe who drops by to sit with me as I munch my bagel while fishing.

"Hiya, kid!" His grin is twice the size of mine.

"Ah, Mr. Ruth, how very nice to see you. Wasn't sure I'd get to again. Life is good, Babe, I must say. But, without you, I don't know where I'd be right now. I might have a trophy sturgeon, but I'd never have met Karen. Or pocketed such a lovely fee. I owe you big, big fella."

"No, Ovid, you owe me nothing. I owe you."

"Whadaya mean, Babe?"

"I got my bonus from the Boss."

"For?"

"For the idea you had about me talking to your old man. The Boss loved it. Didn't explain why but it tickled him pink. By the way, I'm glad I got to meet Bernie. We had a nice talk and I put your question to him. He gave me a message for you."

"You met my father?" I say, sitting up, wide-eyed. "What did he say?"

"I'll *show* you what he said." With a gleeful look, he moves his thick left fist toward me. As it approaches, it takes on a more natural color, much less ghostly than the rest of him.

Seeing my look of surprise he says, "Been bumped up a Proto notch."

Before I can replay, he turns up his fist and slowly opens it. In it is a folded slip of paper. I stare at him, then at the paper.

"What are you looking at?" he says, laughing. "Take it!" He waggles it in my face.

I take the paper, but can't take my eyes off him.

"Well, aren't you going to read it?"

"Sure I am, Babe," I say, "but you just broke the wall."

"That's what I've been trying to show you, Ovid. I'm getting the hang of materializing. Now, are you going to read this damn thing or do I have to read it to you?"

I unfold the paper and read it. I can't speak for what seems like a minute. Then I recite to him the simple words it contains.

Do what you think is right. I love you. Dad.

I recognize the small, carefully scripted bookkeeper's handwriting. Then I read the words again. And again. And again.

Do what you think is right. I love you. Dad.

"Thank you, Babe," I say, hoarsely. I knuckle away some tears. "Can you tell me any more about him?" He shakes his head no. I guess that's how the System works. I nod my understanding.

I reach out to shake the Babe's hand. He breaks the wall again to reach out for mine. His grip is like iron. This is the first time I've felt his physical being. I think of all the times he's gripped a bat this way.

"You don't know what this means to me, Babe. I just don't

really know how to thank you."

"I told you, you don't have to," he says. "But how about one of those bagel things and a cuppa joe? Black. And while you're at it, one of your lovely stogies, and, if you have anything to pour other than that rotgut you drink yourself, some of that too."

These requests are gladly met. I dredge up some ancient Haig & Haig Pinch and pour him four fingers. "Ice?" No, he likes it neat. We talk away the morning; about baseball, about the way things were in his day, about what it was like to be the Babe. He asks for seconds of everything. I've rarely spent such fascinating hours.

I offer him a third scotch. He waves it off, reconsiders, then waves it back on. There we sit decadently sipping at high noon. Don't know how his is affecting him, but mine's got me a little goofy.

Then the two of us, the friends we've become, make our farewells.

"I'd give ya a big hug, Ovid, but I haven't got the hang of *fully* materializing yet."

"Hey, Babe, there's one last favor I'd like to ask of you. It's important. It's for John Blackstone."

"Ask away," he says, his hands resting on his ample belly.

So I ask. He nods his assurance that he'll comply.

Then we shake again, and Georgehermanbaberuth is gone, never to materialize in my life again.

50.

I sit back in my lounger and think about the past few days. For twenty minutes I don't move. Then I read Bernie's message a few more times. As I read it a fourth time, it disappears, evanesces, just like the Babe himself. I no longer have any proof that it—or the Babe—ever really existed. In my life or in his afterlife. I look at his empty coffee cup and rocks glass, but I'm willing to bet there are no prints on them except mine.

Finally, I pull out my mother's now-wrinkled and stained calling card. I've been carrying it around in my pocket all week.

I stare at the card for a full minute.

My cell is sitting on the table next to me.

I reach for it.

It is near midnight at Overlook. John Blackstone sits upright in his bed, manipulating his handheld over his newest game, R.B.1 Baseball 17. He has been playing for the past several hours. Baseball players run about the field on its screen. He hears a gentle knock on his door. He is too involved to acknowledge the knock.

The knock grows louder and more impatient.

"Who's there?" he mumbles in his signature monotone.

"It's me, Babe Ruth."

"Come in, Mr. Ruth." John says, continuing to work the R.B.1 Baseball 17 buttons. "You're up next."

The Babe enters.

Made in the USA
Las Vegas, NV
10 December 2021

36995738R00134